Flight to Oblivion

John Hash

Flight to Oblivion is a work of fiction. Any resemblance of a character or characters to any person, living or dead, is unintentional and co-incidental.

Other books by John L. Hash

Honey Branches: The Meade Estate
Starkeeper
Lero's Mission
Go Get Nadja

Copyright 2014

ISBN 978-0-9831685-4-6

Published in the United States by

Wiltshire Books

Huntington, West Virginia

This book is dedicated to God,
Who watches over us all.

Flight to Oblivion

Chapter 1

"Clearance Delivery, MAS 370. Good morning."

"MAS 370 stand by. Malaysia Six is cleared to Frankfurt via AGOSA Alpha Departure, six thousand feet. Squawk two one zero six."

"MAS 370 request level."

"MAS 370, we are ready, requesting flight level three five zero to Beijing."

"MAS 370 is cleared to Beijing via PIBOS A Departure. Six thousand feet. Squawk two one five seven."

(Note: "PIBOS A" is a reference to a standard instrument departure, a procedure that, if followed, will guide the pilot to a particular place or route after take-off. Air traffic control uses SIDs to organize departures at busy airports.)

"Beijing, Pibos A, six thousand, squawk two one five seven. MAS 370, thank you."

"MAS 370 you are welcome. Over to ground."

"Good day."

"Ground, MAS 370. Good morning. Charlie One, requesting push and start."

"MAS 370, Lumpur ground, Good morning. Push back and start approved. Runway 32 Right. Exit via Sierra 4 POB 239 Mike Romeo Oscar.

"Read back correct."

"MAS 370, requesting taxi."

"MAS 370, taxi to holding point Alpha 11, Runway 32 Right, via standard route. Hold short of Bravo."

"Alpha 11 Standard route, Hold short of Bravo, MAS 370."

"MAS 370, Tower."

"Tower, MAS 370, Good Morning."

"MAS 370, good morning. Lumpur Tower. Holding point Alpha 11, Runway 32 right."

"Line up 32 Right, Alpha 10, MAS 370."

"MAS 370 32 Right. Cleared for Take off. Good night."

"32 Right, Cleared for Takeoff, MAS 370. Thank you. Bye"

"Departure, Malaysian 370."

"Malaysian 370, Climb flight level one eight zero, direct AGARI, cancel SID."

"Malaysian 370, Okay, level one eight zero, contact Lumpur Radar on one three two six."

"One three two point six, Malaysian three Seven Zero. Good night."

"Lumpur control, Malaysian three seven zero."

"Malaysian three seven zero, Lumpur radar. Good morning. Climb flight level two five zero.

"Morning, level two five zero, Malaysian Three Seven Zero."

"Malaysian three seven zero, climb to flight level three five zero."

"Flight level three five zero, Malaysian three seven zero."

"Malaysian Three seven zero, maintaining level three five zero."

"Malaysian three seven zero, contact Ho Chi Minh one twenty decimal niner. Good night."

"Good night, Malaysian Three seven zero."

Chapter 2

Captain Sabah looked over at First Officer Shah. They nodded to each other. First Officer Shah reached up to the cabin pressure control and dialed it to zero. The indicator rapidly changed from indicating a cabin pressure equivalent to four thousand feet MSL to thirty five thousand feet. He and Captain Sabah reached for their quick donning oxygen masks. Behind the flight deck bulkhead, the pressure reduced, over a period of twenty seconds, from that found at four thousand feet above sea level to the pressure found at thirty five thousand feet. Cold air flooded the cabin. The temperature dropped to minus fifty degrees Fahrenheit in the same twenty seconds. Those who realized what was happening just had time to realize what was happening before they lost consciousness. It all took less than two minutes. In five minutes, there was not a living soul in the passenger cabin.

Captain Sabah and First Officer Shah brought the pressure back up to normal, took off their masks and reprogrammed the flight director (autopilot) to altitude hold and a heading of two one zero. The Boeing 777 began a graceful turn to the left.

In twelve minutes, they turned the big aircraft to a new heading of two eight five degrees over the Straits of Malacca and motored into the night.

The new heading would take them south of the Indian sub-continent by about three hundred miles, well clear of any land based radar.

Twenty minutes later, Ho Chi Minh Radar called: "Malaysian 370, Ho Chi Minh radar."

After another minute or so, they called again: "Malaysian 370, Ho Chi Minh radar."

Another minute or so passed, then "Malasian 370, Ho Chi Minh radar."

Senior Flight controller Nuyen, called to the supervisor, "Malaysian 370 does not answer. Should we call Lumpur radar by telephone?"

Supervisor Cao lifted his telephone and dialed the number for Lumpur radar. It rang five rings before anyone answered.

"Lumpur radar, Major Abadan speaking."

"Major Abadan, this is Supervisor Cao at Ho Chi Minh radar. We cannot contact your Malaysian flight 370. Did it depart normally?"

"Yes," said Major Abadan, it departed a few minutes late, but we handed it off about twenty minutes ago at flight level three five zero. It was told to contact your facility on one two zero decimal niner. We will try to contact it on frequencies available to us. If we contact Flight 370, we will report back to you by land line. Thank you for your concern."

"You are welcome, Major Abadan. I hope there is nothing wrong. Good night."

Major Abadan hung up the telephone and spoke to his shift supervisor: "Keep trying to contact Flight 370 on all frequencies you used for him tonight. Is there another flight in his vicinity that we might enlist to try to contact him?"

"Cathay Pacific Flight Fifty Four is about one hundred nautical miles southwest of 370's last known position, at flight level three three zero. I will contact them and see if they can raise 370."

By this time, Abadan had left his supervisor's desk and come to the console where Ibrahim Mahmoud sat. He was the last controller to have talked to the pilots of Flight 370.

He said: "Ho Chi Minh radar reports no contact with Malaysian Flight 370. Try to raise them on any frequency you can and contact any flight in its vicinity to see if they can raise them."

Abadan stepped to his desk and lifted the telephone, and dialed again.

"Malaysian Air dispatch," answered the voice.

"This is Major Abadan at Lumpur Radar. We cannot contact your flight 370. We continue to try. Ho Chi Minh radar reports no contact on their end, either. Contact me at this number if you have any contact or advice for us."

"Will do, Major Abadan. Thank you for the call."

"Major, Cathay fifty four reports no response to their calls."

"Thank you, Nuyen. Keep trying."

After fifteen minutes, Major Abadan again lifted the telephone and dialed.

"Malasian Department of Transport, Captain Amar speaking."

"Captain Amar, this is Major Abadan at Lumpur Radar. We have lost contact with Malaysian Flight 370. Ho Chi Minh radar reports no contact either after our hand off about half an hour ago."

"Very well, Major Abadan. We appreciate the heads up. We will alert all aircraft and radars under our control to be on the lookout. Someone from our office will contact you shortly to coordinate a search for the plane. I have your number, so we will call you at that number. Thank you, again."

By now all ships and airplanes in the area where Flight 370 disappeared were calling on their radios and squinting at their radar displays to get a glimpse of the plane. The frequencies were strangely silent and the screens gave no clues.

Within an hour, the word got out to the news services and it went viral around the world in a matter of minutes. Malaysian 370 was missing.

Chapter 3

"Good Evening, Memphis Center, Jones speaking."

"Jonesy, this is Gable at Federal Express. I need to file an international flight plan.

"Sure thing. Ready to copy."

"FedEx Flight 513, departing Singapore at 1030 UTC, Aircraft is a Boeing 747 Freighter, Landing Karachi, Jinnah Airport, N number is N375FE, Equipment code is Golf, Fuel for sixteen hours. Two souls on board. The usual Jet Routes. Need anything else?

"Nope, got it. Will file right away. Thanks."

Colonel Gilano of the ISI, smiled as he hung up.

In a few minutes, the teletype at Jinnah Approach Control clacked off the arrival flight plan for Flight 513. ETA was 1800 local time. The afternoon shift controllers in the tower made a "boat" for Flight 513 when they had slack time during the shift. (A "boat" is what the controllers call the piece of plastic that has the flight number on it, along with type, and is stacked in a sloped open table with other boats for incoming flights. As the aircraft approaches and is "worked" the boat will be passed from approach ((or RADAR, as international airports call it)) to Tower controllers for landing instructions.)

Major Milar made sure that all the normal technicians and painters were assigned to other work outside of the Ispahani hangar that night and the next day. Now, all the personnel were ISI cleared technicians and knew the plan.

Several hours later, midst the flood of lights and the crowded microphones, Sahendra Suo, Chief Executive Officer of Malaysian Airlines, stepped tentatively to a position behind a podium at corporate headquarters in Kuala Lumpur.

"Ladies and Gentlemen, I regret to inform you that our flight MH370 has disappeared under very mysterious circumstances. There were two hundred sixty eight persons on board, including a flight crew of ten. The aircraft, a Boeing seven seven seven, departed regularly, on time, from Kuala Lumpur approximately six hours ago. It reported normally in flight to our air traffic controllers until it was handed off to Ho Chi Minh approach over the Malacca Straits on its way to Beijing, China. Controllers at Ho Chi Minh approach tried several times to contact the aircraft with no success. Radar tracking indicates that , for reasons unknown to us, the aircraft made a left turn to a southwesterly heading and crossed our territory to a position southwest of our country, then, based on analysis of reports through the ACARS reporting system, it appears that the aircraft proceeded southwesterly out over the Indian Ocean. We continue to call to the aircraft and every air traffic controller within a thousand miles is calling to it continually. We do not know what caused this change in course and we do not know where this aircraft is. A wide ranging search is under way and we will report to you any information we acquire. Our thought and prayers go out to the relatives and loved ones of the passengers and crew."

Suo stepped away from the microphones and out of the glare of the lights. He walked solemnly off the stage with tears streaming down his face. He felt a combination of grief for the passengers and crew and their loved ones and an embarrassing loss of face for his company.

Chapter 4

According to the Jinnah Radar control station log, Flight 513 first called in at 1722.

"Jinnah Radar, FedEx Flight 513 with you level at three one zero. Good afternoon."

"Good afternoon, Flight 513, Jinnah radar, squawk 2134 for us please. Information Delta is current."

"Two one three four and Delta for Flight 513. Thanks."

"Five one three, you are in radar contact. Plan descent to one zero, ten thousand feet in twenty minutes. We show you two hundred ten DME from Jinnah." (DME stands for Distance Measuring Equipment. It can tell the radar operator and the pilot the distance of an aircraft from a navigation radio and its airspeed.)

"Thank you, Jinnah Radar. Five one three will expect to begin descent to one zero, ten thousand feet, in eighteen minutes."

In a few minutes, Jinnah Radar broadcast: "Flight 513, descend and maintain one zero, ten thousand feet, contact Jinnah Approach now on one two five decimal seven. Good afternoon."

"Thank you, Jinnah Radar. Five one three over to Jinnah Approach on one two five decimal seven. Good afternoon."

"Jinnah Approach, Fed Ex Flight 513, with you, descending out of sixteen thousand for one zero, ten thousand feet, squawking two one three four, with Delta."

"Good afternoon, Fed Ex five one three, Jinnah Approach. Report level at one zero, ten thousand. We show you fifty four DME."

"Thank you, Jinnah Approach, Five one three is now level at one zero, ten thousand."

"Roger, Five one three, fly heading of three five zero, begin descent to six thousand feet, report reaching."

"Five one three out of one zero, ten thousand for six. Will report."

After a few minutes, "Jinnah Approach, Five one three is level at six thousand."

"Roger, five one three, Contact Jinnah tower on one one eight decimal five. Good afternoon."

"Five one three over to tower on one one eight decimal five. Good afternoon."

"Jinnah Tower, Fed Ex Flight five one three."

"Good afternoon, Fed Ex Flight five one three, you are second to land following Lufthansa DC-10 on short final. Continue. Expect Runway Seven right, eleven thousand five hundred feet available."

"Thank you, Jinnah Tower. Five one three expects Runway Seven right, looking for the traffic, yes, have him now on short final."

Lots was happening on Five one three just now. Flaps were extending, landing gear coming down. There were none of the usual flight attendant briefings. None of the hustle and bustle of two hundred fifty passengers sitting upright and tightening their seat belts for the long looked-forward-to landing. The cabin was completely quiet.

"Five one three, cleared to land, Runway Seven right."

"Roger, Five one three understands clear to land, Seven right."

The huge Boeing 777 swept up to the runway threshold, transitioning from a level attitude to nose up as it made the last few hundred yards of its approach. Six big tires on each main gear moaned as they accelerated from still to one hundred ten knots in a second. Each tire left a long black streak on the runway and then rolled under the weight of the huge aircraft.

"Five one three, contact ground, point niner, when clear."

"Roger, Tower, good to be with you, five one three."

"Jinnah Ground, Fed Ex Flight 513 with you, off Runway seven right, taxi to Ispahani hangar, please."

"Roger, Flight five one three, taxi to Ispahani hangar via taxiway Juliet and Alpha."

"Thank you, five one three."

No one noticed that it was a Boeing 777, rather than the Boeing 747 that was listed in the flight plan, or, if they noticed, they disregarded it.

The huge plane taxied as directed and as it drew up to the hangar, about fifty feet short, it cut its engines and the pilots prepared to disembark.

A tug attached its connection to the nose landing gear and began towing the plane into the huge hangar. As soon as the wings passed through the opening, the doors began to close from each side. By the time the empennage had passed through, the doors were only ten feet from each tip. Within thirty seconds of the empennage passing through, the doors were completely shut. Armed guards stepped out of the service door and stationed themselves around the hangar, at each corner and each door.

Colonel Rawal of the ISI, directed the squad of technicians: "Go aboard, remove the bodies and all their baggage, prepare the interior for another flight. Place the bodies and their baggage in the refrigerated trucks for transport."

"Yes sir," said the lead technician and the men moved toward the stairs toward the doors of the aircraft.

Captain Sahab and First Officer Shah came down the stairs and greeted Rawal.

"Everything go according to plan?" asked Rawal.

"Yes,sir. No problems. With your permission, we will get some rest and be ready for the next leg."

"Good idea. Captain Faoud, show the pilots to their quarters so they may rest."

"Yes, sir," said Faoud and led the two pilots out.

The north west corner of the hangar held several rooms for use as offices and quiet rooms for resting pilots. As they entered their quiet room, Faoud turned on the lights for the pilots and went over to the air conditioning controls and set them to bring the temperature down to a comfortable level.

As First Officer Shah closed the door to the hall, Faoud walked back toward the door. When he got within eight feet, or so, of the pilots, he drew his pistol and shot them both. As they dropped to the floor, he shot each of them again to be certain they were dead. Then he left the room and locked the door.

Chapter 5

After the pilots left on their way to their sleeping quarters, Major Rawal met with the paint crew.

"Begin immediately to paint the colors and logo of Federal Express over the present paint of the aircraft. You must be finished in six hours. I will try to keep other crews out of your way. Report any problems."

Captain Ahmed Dissi saluted and turned promptly to gather his men and get started.

In about half an hour, a military cargo truck pulled up to the hangar. Its driver and another man got out and went inside. An armed guard watched over the truck while they went inside.

They showed their IDs to the guard just outside the door. He directed them to the office that Major Rawal had taken over.

"Captain Ahmed and crew, reporting as ordered, sir," said Ahmed as he stood before Rawal and saluted.

"Good to have you here, Ahmed. Follow me."

He led Ahmed into a private office. Once they were sure there was no one who could overhear them, Rawal asked: "Which ordnance did you bring?"

"I have three KL7 devices, sir. We have trucked them from the depot in Rawalpindi. My men need rest, but you can begin unloading the devices as soon as you want."

"Good. Have your men get some rest in the sleeping quarters here in the hangar. Another crew will take over and unload your truck. You may stay or rest as you wish. Nicely done, Ahmed. Congratulations," said Rawal.

Now the hangar was buzzing with activity, with the crew removing the bodies and putting them into the transport trucks for disposal at sea, the paint crew busy changing the appearance of the aircraft, and Rawal's crew unloading the devices from Ahmed's truck and placing them in the cargo holds of the plane. Now the remaining arrival was the last major expected group.

Chapter 6

There was a sound. Definitely a sound. Lero stirred. The first thing he realized was that Jean was softly breathing on his neck. She was lying on top of him. If felt so wonderful. Her soft breasts were pressed against his chest. The point of her left hip was pushing into his belly between the point of his right hip and his belly button. He said a silent prayer of thanksgiving for Jean. She was so good to him and so good for him. Yet, there was still the sound. It was a buzzing sound. He thought for a while and then realized that it was his cell phone in the pocket of his shirt which was hanging on the chair across the room. The screen on the phone was lit and he could see it through the cloth of the shirt. It must have been the middle of the night. He had been asleep for some time. He thought that he would wait and see if the phone would stop, but it did not. He finally decided to stir and get up and see who was calling. He gently rolled Jean onto her side and she awoke as he did so. She moaned softly and reached for him. He whispered to her: "The phone is ringing. I'll be right back." He crossed the room and punched the send button on the phone.

"Hello," he said.

"Please hold for Mr. Murfree," the female voice said.

"Alright," he said, but he got no reply.

In a few seconds, a voice said, "This is Mr. Murfree. Say the word."

Lero knew that he was talking with the President. He responded: "Houston."

Now the President knew that he was indeed talking to Lero, and Lero knew that he was talking to the President.

"Sorry to call so untimely. Can you function without restriction?"

"Yes, sir," said Lero. "What do you need me to do, sir?"

"I need you and Jean immediately. There is a car waiting in your driveway. Please come right away. Bring only barest necessities. Time is critical. The officer waiting for you will take you where I can talk to you more securely. Please hurry."

"Yes, sir. Give us a couple of minutes. We were sound asleep."

"Good enough. Thanks. Talk to you again in a while."

He hung up. By now Jean had heard Lero's side of the conversation and had sat up on the side of the bed. She was so beautiful in the dim light.

"Mr. Murfree wants us both to go with an officer who has a car sitting in our driveway. He says it is urgent. Please get dressed quickly," he said as he pulled on his shorts and reached for his socks. In two minutes, they were fully dressed. They left the house and found a black Ford sedan backed into their driveway. The officer standing beside it opened the back door for them and got himself into the car with one smooth motion. He pulled away without a word and sped through the dark streets. After he had gone a couple of blocks, Lero could see over the driver's shoulder to see that they were going ninety miles an hour. In a few seconds, the officer flashed the bright lights a couple of times and a chain link fence began to open on rollers. Just as it provided enough room for the car, they shot through the gate. The car had slowed considerably by now, but was still going briskly. As it arced to the right and came to a stop, Lero and Jean saw that he had pulled up to a Lear Jet that sat darkly on the tarmac. As they opened the door, the door to the jet opened and a young woman in uniform came out to help them aboard. They could hear that the off side engine was running and as they climbed the stairs to board, the pilots started the number one engine on their side of the plane. At the direction of the young woman, they tumbled into leather seats and buckled up. By this time, the aircraft had reached the threshold of the runway and it turned onto it and went to full throttle without hesitation. Lero and Jean were pushed back into their seats by the takeoff thrust. In about twelve seconds, the jet left the runway and sprang into the night.

Once the Lear began to level off, the flight attendant brought a lap top computer to them and sat it on the table in front of their seats. It had been turned on and was booting. When it came up with a screen, it was blue with the seal of the President of the United States on it. In a few seconds, the face of President Thompson appeared. Through the speakers he spoke to them.

"Sorry to have awakened you both and hustled you off in such a hurry, but this is an urgent situation and I need your help."

"About twelve hours ago, a Boeing 777 enroute from Kuala Lumpur to Beijing disappeared from radar just after it was handed off to Ho Chi Minh Radar in Vietnam. At the time, the aircraft was about eighty nautical miles off the Vietnam coast. I will fill you in on the details later, but we think the plane may have been commandeered and flown to an Islamic country as part of a terror plot."

"This is for your ears and eyes only. We think the aircraft is in the Ispahani Hangar on Jinnah Airport in Karachi, Pakistan. We suspect that it is being altered and loaded with nuclear and/or chemical weapons. We are in no position to know what the plans of the terrorist group are, but we have to be ready to act no matter whom they intend to attack."

"Our response will depend on who is in control. We think it could be any one or more of several groups, none of which are eaten up with the milk of human kindness. If it is the Chechens, they may be intending to hit Moscow. In a perverse way, that could be worse than hitting us. The Russians would not think twice about unleashing their entire missile defense arsenal at the perceived aggressor, which they might just think is us. That prospect is very scary."

"If it is Hezbollah, they could be planning to hit Israel or us. If it is Hamas, the most likely target is Israel, but on the other hand, it they are arming the plane with chemical or biological weapons, even if they hit Jerusalem directly, it would probably kill everyone in the west bank and Gaza, too. If they arm the plane with a nuclear weapon, it would be more likely they would hit Tel Aviv, if the controllers are indeed Hamas. We have to keep in mind that if it is either Hamas or Hezbollah, Iran is pulling some strings, too.

If the people who have the aircraft are Pakistani nationalists, they may be planning to hit India, somewhere with lots of people, like Mumbai or Calcutta. India is the most populous democracy on the planet. Pakistanis and Indians do not get along well, even after almost eighty years of separation. I guess the disputed area of Kashmir keeps them at each other."

"If the controllers are Al Qaeda, the target will most likely be America or Great Britain. Great Britain helped us more than anybody else in Afghanistan, remember, and we have to keep in mind in our analysis that these people are driven by a revenge motive."

"On the other hand, since the airplane is in Karachi, it is doubtless under the temporary control of the ISI. That means there could be a plot conceived by the Taliban, maybe working with Al Qaeda. We have our best people brainstorming this problem. The CIA Antiterrorism Division is fully staffed around the clock. DIA and NSA and CIA are at full alert."

"We have numerous assets in Karachi, but none with any way of getting onto the airport other than in the passenger terminal. We are working on that and will advise."

"I am sending you two now because I cannot wait for larger bureaucracies to mobilize and get moving. I need "eyes on" this problem. Jefe will try to catch up with you, but he is way behind you all right now. I will keep him updated, but you are in charge. I will give you an operation code name soon, but right now the important thing is to get you to a position from which you can coordinate our response to this threat. This is a genuine emergency. I need you both direly. I am so glad you could be available."

"I know you got yanked out of a very comfortable situation. The Lear jet you are riding in will rendezvous with a B-1 at Vandenberg Air Force Base. The B-1 will take you at maximum speed to an island off the coast of India where a Carrier Onboard Delivery will take you out to the Reagan that we will use as our forward control location as long as our plans stay consistent with those now in place. Jean will be met in Mumbai by a P-8 Poseidon and will fly with them to monitor el-int and sig-int during this operation."

(Note: These are references to electrical intelligence, broadcasts of voice transmissions or signals intelligence, which are broadcasts of signals or code or data.)

"I want you both out there close to the problem, so you can help me decide what to do. I am marshalling assets from the region and you will have plenty of help. At the speeds it is capable of, the B-1 will have you to Mumbai in six hours. This thing is unfolding so fast that your arrival there may not be in time, however. I don't want to use the normal response network we have in place because we don't want to be observed going into an alert mode. If the enemy even finds out we are watching, they may bolt and do something rash. If they plan to use this plane against the U.S. homeland, we will have several hours to arrange some sort of interception. If they change plans and decided to hit Tel Aviv or Jerusalem or London or Paris, we won't have much time at all."

"The plane disappeared from radar shortly after one A.M. local time. That would have been Noon your time. They have had several hours already to get ready. They would first have to remove enough of the bodies of the passengers and their luggage to have room and carrying capacity for whatever device or devices they intend to load on board. They will have to repaint the fuselage to disguise it as another carrier's aircraft. They will have to service and refuel the plane, too. We think, even with large crews attending each task, it is going to take them at least twelve hours to get ready. The whole world is looking for this aircraft, but they are mostly looking for it in the southern Indian Ocean where the local authorities have told the public they think it went down. The ACARS home office in Murrayville, California, has found that the onboard ACARS system transmitted return pings to the land based system for six hours after the plane disappeared. Luckily for us, the NSA has been monitoring the ACARS system for some time and was able to receive the same data in real time, so they were on top of this immediately. The Doppler data indicates that it is just as possible that the jet took a northwesterly course after turning off its transponder and ACARS system, as it is possible that it took a southerly course to a position about a thousand miles west of Perth, Australia. More on this later."

"According to my information, your aircraft is talking to Vandenberg Approach Control just now. You should be on the ground there in a few minutes. Once you are on the B-1 and aloft, they will reconnect us so we can discuss our options. Again, thank you both for being there for us. Jean, the wide band scanner you designed and built is on the

B-1 and we will transfer it to a P-8 Poseidon once we get you both to Mumbai, so you can be aloft and monitoring all of the radio and sig-int for us with it."

"I will talk to you again in a few minutes."

As the President hung up, they could hear and feel the first notch of flaps come out. The plane decelerated markedly and in a minute or so, the landing gear deployed. The pilot made a good landing and taxied rapidly to the end of the runway. The pilots shut down the port engine, next to the door, but did not shut down the starboard engine. The Lear Jet came to a stop next to the B-1. Lero and Jean hastily got out of the Lear Jet and trotted, hand in hand, the fifty yards to the stairs of the B-1. As soon as they were on board, the stairs were pulled away and the door closed and the wheels started rolling. The pilots started the near side engines on the roll. Lero and Jean were directed to seats by a corpsman (actually corpswoman, in this case) in Air Force uniform. Within a few seconds after they fastened their seat belts, they felt the massive thrust of the engines spooling up for take-off. Lero tried to reach out to the seat in front to twist so he could look out the window, but could not do so. The thrust was too much. They had been on the ground for less than six minutes.

Chapter 7

ACARS is headquartered in Annapolis, Maryland, with regional offices in London and Singapore.

In the radio room of the USS Reagan, one of America's newest nuclear aircraft carriers, the satellite feed began to print. Chief Boatswain's Mate Schaffer tore off the paper, put it in a sealed envelope, wrote "Captain Warshovsky, Eyes Only," on it and called to his courier, Seaman first class Orser.

"Take this to the Captain in CIC, on the double."

"Sure chief," said Orser, took the envelope and set out at a brisk pace.

When Captain Warshovsky opened the envelope, he let his Exec, Commander Smythe, look over his shoulder. Both were startled by the message: "This is NO DRILL. Break. Break. Proceed at once, all possible speed to 23 degrees, zero minutes, zero seconds North Latitude, sixty seven degrees zero minutes, zero seconds East longitude, and stand by for further orders. Update to follow by data link. CINCPAC."

"Mr. Murdock, pipe the bridge. Order them to come right to three five zero degrees and go to all ahead full. Will come to the bridge forthwith."

Lieutenant Murdock did as ordered. In a few subtle seconds everyone on board could feel a change in direction and a surge of power.

"Note the time in the log, Mr. Parsons," said the Captain to his Officer of the Deck.

Within a couple of minutes, the same order went out to the Commanding officers of the guided Missile Frigate Reuben James and the Nuclear Submarine Utah. More than five thousand men were on their way to the point designated, which was a spot in the Indian Ocean about four hundred west of the northern Indian coast, south of Pakistan.

In the CIA Counter Terrorism Center, over a period of hours beginning with when the flight failed to contact Ho Chi Minh Radar after the handoff, the amount of personnel present and the intensity of activity had increased markedly. Television screens were feeding commercial television coverage of the mysterious disappearance and the feeds from branches and technicians were also displayed. The screen that captured everyone's attention was the analysis of the ACARS pings to the aircraft every hour and the responses. The airline had not paid

for the full subscription to ACARS, so the only feed
would have been from the feature called Classic
Aero, which was a much simpler service that only
reported basic information rather than the full report
of parameters from the aircraft available with a full
ACARS subscription. By analyzing the Doppler
changes in the pings to and from the aircraft, the
equipment was able to infer a distance from stations
and plot possible positions of the aircraft when it
gave its abbreviated response to the pings. The
display showed two possible courses, one toward
the southwest from the point where the handoff
failed to take place, and the other to the west north
west which would carry the flight over or close to
India and beyond.

The commercial television stations consistently
broadcast the fuel capacity of the Boeing 777-
200ER as 31,000 gallons and its range at 5235
nautical miles with full fuel. The men were
perplexed as to why this erroneous information was
consistently broadcast. Many surmised that
someone in control deliberately fed the incorrect
information to the television networks to conceal the
fact that the Boeing 777-200ER could hold 45,220
gallons of fuel and had a range of 7,725 nautical
miles, or more than eight thousand eight hundred
statute miles. Technicians were busy plotting this
radius onto the plot of the possible courses taken by
the airliner. A trend was clear. Either the plane flew
out over the southern Indian Ocean or it went
toward the west north west. A track in that direction
could take it to Azerbaijan, Turkministan,

Afghanistan, Pakistan or elsewhere. This was beginning to pucker all those who watched the plots come in on an hourly basis.

Over at NSA, even the Director was at the center throughout the night. They had the capability of monitoring the email traffic of the Malaysian Department of Transport which had primary responsibility for the investigation. They could also listen to selected telephone conversations and record them.

Talking heads on television were coming up with all sorts of theories about what happened to the airplane and its passengers. Most often quoted theories included a catastrophic decompression at thirty five thousand feet, the last reported altitude of the jet, pilot takeover and diversion, or a hijacking by a passenger or stowaway. One of the techs posed the question on the screen: "Could the aircraft have been struck by a meteorite, or a piece of falling space debris, causing the decompression?" No one was laughing at the possibility because there were two hundred sixty nine souls on board, but still, their main concern was the possible use of the plane for a terror strike. After all, it had a range of more than eight thousand statute miles and could carry anything that they could get into it.

The Directors of the CIA and the NSA have conferred and agreed to feed each other all information either had on the situation, so there was plenty of information. It was just that the information pouring into each center did not tell very much.

All eyes in the Counterterrorism center were focused on the feed showing that the flight path pointed toward Karachi, Pakistan. A layout diagram of Jinnah Airport showed a large hangar on the southwest corner of the airport. It was a service hangar that was capable of holding the largest commercial and military aircraft. The Ispahani hangar was well known in aviation circles for its size and how busy it was.

Chapter 8

Lero stirred. The deceleration awoke him. Bright
sunlight streamed into the tiny window to his left.
The cabin was now lighted internally since the
windows were so small. Jean soon awakened, too.
The corpswoman, who had been asleep in a nearby
seat, had been alerted through her earphones that
the first aerial refueling was about to take place.
The B-1 needed to decelerate from Mach 2.1 to
three hundred knots and descend from its altitude of
Flight level Five eight zero to flight level two four
zero to rendezvous with the KC-10 tanker. As a very
experienced pilot, Lero could tell what was going on
and he looked out the small window to get a glimpse
of the seascape.

The corpswoman saw him move and came over to
them both.

"As soon as we finish refueling, I will get us some
breakfast. It will be a few minutes. Please wait until
we finish refueling to visit the lavatory. Keep your
seat belts on for now. Good morning."

Lero nodded his acknowledgement and smiled at
her.

He saw the KC-10 below them and to his side of the
B-1 for just a moment before it was out of sight. By
now the B-1 had decelerated and was leveling at

Flight Level two four zero. Lero knew that the crew was paying close attention to the interception of the KC-10 and that refueling would begin soon. It only took about ten minutes. Then, with a slight descent, the B-1 pulled free of the KC-10 and he got a glimpse of it to the left as they pulled away. In about ten seconds, he felt the mighty thrust of the B-1's four engines go back to MAX CRUISE setting and he was plastered back in his seat as they climbed back to altitude. In just a few minutes, he felt the B-1 begin to level off and it accelerated again. Once it stabilized, he saw the corpswoman put her hand to her headset to aid reception of a message from the flight deck. She spoke into her mike, but he could not hear or discern what she said. She then unplugged her headset and came over to them.

"You can visit the lavatory now. I will have some breakfast for you shortly. Scrambled eggs and sausage with orange juice and coffee."

Lero nodded and said "Thanks." He helped Jean to her feet and held onto her until she indicated she was steady enough to walk. Then he released her and watched her walk to the lavatory. Just watching her walk stirred something in him. He said a silent prayer of thanksgiving.

When she came back from the lavatory, he took his turn. As he took his seat, she asked: "What do you think based on the President's brief?"

He said: "They seem to have covered most all the probabilities, but I can think of one they did not touch on. Maybe it was just because of the rush, but they did not mention ISIS or ISIL. They are different names for the same group. It has been a surprise to most analysts that it has coalesced so quickly into a cohesive fighting group. I suspect that most of the officer corps consists of former Syrian and Iraqi Army officers. Our analysts don't miss much. I bet they warned the previous administration about this and the previous administration stuck its head in the sand and ignored the threat in its urgency to get us out of Iraq. With all the material we abandoned in Iraq, they would be able to arm themselves quickly. Complete withdrawal from Iraq was a huge blunder. Now, if we ever want to go back into Iraq, we will have to fight our way in again and manufacture the tanks and MRAPs and munitions and infrastructure necessary. It was such a waste. These people only had to wait until we left to grab all our equipment. It was so stupid to leave in such haste that we did not negotiate a status of forces agreement and leave some troops there to prevent just this kind of situation. The higher ups in the previous administration just didn't seem to understand these people at all. They were so intent on fulfilling their ill-advised promises to withdraw from Iraq that they did not remove our equipment as they fled, either. It was a formula for disaster. It boggles the mind to think of all the miscues, mistakes and blunders we have committed in Iraq. When the Iraqi people thanked us for toppling

Saddam Hussein and then asked us to go home, we should have done it."

"With the Rockefellers and their ilk in league with the Saudis through the Saudi Aramco Oil complex and with the Rockefellers' oil companies, Exxon-Mobil, and the like having a forty percent market share in our country, even though they have only about six percent of the world's oil, we are way too influenced by the Saudis, too," said Jean.

Lero nodded. "I have a feeling that this airplane situation is just the opening chapter in a much larger theatre of operations. Pretty scary."

She nodded and they turned their attention to eggs and bacon.

Chapter 9

The SS Nederlander plowed through the four foot
swells of a rainy Mediterranean night. The ship
wallowed a bit as it progressed. It was three bells on
the midnight watch, one thirty AM local time for
civilians. In the center hold, three men were tugging
at containers that had been lashed to pallets which
were, in turn, lashed to the deck with straps through
the loops welded into the deck. They worked quickly
in the dark, with the only illumination being their
forehead mounted short range flashlights. One of
them wore the uniform of the United Nations
Peacekeeping force and he did not do enough
actual work to stain his uniform with sweat, so as to
avoid suspicion later. The other two labored
strenuously. Each drum was rolled on its rim over
to a position next to the hatch in the side of the ship.
Each drum then had a flotation collar attached with
attached inflatable buoy. When they had wrestled
two entire pallets totaling twenty drums to the hatch,
they detached the pallets from which they had come
and brought them to the hatch as well.

While the uniformed man stood watch with his FAL
rifle held at the ready at the entry hatch on the aft
bulkhead, the other two wrestled each drum to the
open hatch and pitched it into the water. There was
so much background noise from the rush of water
and the laboring engines, that no one would notice
what was going on unless they just happeded to be

leaning over the rail above as this was taking place. No one was.

The drums assumed their ordinal positions in a line that was about a thousand feet long by the time they dumped them all. Then they threw the pallets into the Mediterranean and closed the hatch. The two laborers went with the third man out the aft hatch. The soldier resumed his watch in the corridor and the laborers went to their crew compartment to get some sleep.

On board the Syrian Navy Ship Aegli, the officer of the deck noticed the blip on the radar of the marker beacon on the first drum that had been dropped. It was eleven nautical miles ahead, slightly to the right.

"Come right ten degrees, Commander Shora said to the seaman at the wheel.

"Yes, sir, ten degrees right," said the sailor.

Shora went to the bulkhead where the ships telephone hung on a rack. He keyed the transmit button.

"Chief, bring your recovery crew on deck. We are nine miles from the drums."

"Yes, sir," was the prompt answer.

When he reached the bridge, the Chief asked: "How many drums are there, sir?"

"We were told that there would be twenty. We have received no other information."

"Very well, I will have the men ready the nets and gear."

"I will come out and give you a heads up when we get close," said Shora.

The Chief saluted and went down the ladder to the deck.

In forty minutes, the Aegli neared the closest drum. A tiny strobe on its top was flashing. Shora called down to the chief to get his crew ready. Then he ordered the speed reduced to all ahead crawl. Men assembled at the rail with hook poles and nets to retrieve the drums. Once netted, the nets would be hoisted by cranes so they could swing the drums onto the deck. Once on the deck, the hands would put them on two wheel dollies and roll them into a hold where they lashed them down. It took more than two hours to fish out all the drums, but when it was done, they turned the Aegli back to the west and ordered full speed ahead.

Four hours later, the Aegli neared the port of Tartous on the Syrian coast and slipped into a berth in the harbor under cover of darkness. Three large trucks waited by the dock and as soon as the ship was tied down, men began loading the drums onto the trucks. They worked hurriedly and finished in forty minutes. A few minutes later, the trucks lumbered down Route 2 on their way toward Al Shyrat Air Force Base on the road to Homs.

In due time, the trucks arrived at the airbase. When they stopped at the gate, the officer in charge got out and handed his papers to the guards. They quickly waved him into the gates and the trucks lumbered toward the runway. Waiting on the tarmac was an Ilyusian IL-76 transport plane. Once loaded, the doors closed and the pilots signaled to the ground crew that they were ready for engine start. There was no tower from which to seek clearance, so the pilots were in charge of their departure.and they wasted no time getting the airplane to the runway and lined up for takeoff. Their flight plan showed three hours ten minutes to Karachi. Both pilots pushed the power levers to the stop and the transport began its journey into the night.

Chapter 10

General Idris looked carefully at his hand held GPS.
When the coordinates began to get close to the
desired numbers, he signaled the driver to slow
down. Both his SUV and the truck following his SUV
had high flotation tires, so they could travel more
boldly in the desert. It was a starry and moonless
nightscape before them. He knew that the
constantly shifting sands of the Sahara might have
receded or advanced over the bunker since he was
last there. When they were just a few hundredths of
a degree from the desired latitude, he signaled the
driver with a sweep of his hand to slow down even
more.

Finally, when they were quite close to the desired
coordinates, he got out of the truck and went ahead
on foot. By reference to his GPS, he finally came to
the spot he sought. He gave a hand signal to the
men in the following truck and they got out and
came over to where he was. The surface of the
desert looked like the ocean, with small waves in it
as far as they could see. Idris had his driver use a
steel rod, several feet long to probe into the sand.
The first eight feet went in without touching
anything, so the driver pulled the rod out and
screwed another length of rod onto the first and tried
again. At about eleven feet, the rod hit a solid
surface, so they knew how much they had to dig.

The men in the truck had brought light weight digging equipment with them, which they now began to set up. Idris and Shaheen, the man in charge of the other team, went back to their vehicles to wait for the diggers to finish. It took the digging crew an hour and a half to dig out enough sand to reach the bunker. When the head of the digging crew returned to the truck and told them that they had cleared away enough sand, Idris and Shaheen went with him to have a look.

"Yes," said Idris, in French ("Oui"), the language they had in common, that is the correct bunker number above the door. Go ahead and clear a path for the sand sled and connect the winch cables."

The men pulled the truck up within fifty feet of the sloping hole they had dug and got a steel sled about eight feet long and two feet wide out of the truck. They unrolled a stout cable from the winch on the front bumper of the truck and slowly unwound it as they walked it to a spot next to the door they had uncovered.

Idris and Shaheen walked away from the men about twenty yards, so they could talk privately. Idris retrieved a satellite telephone from his SUV and an envelope from his jacket pocket. He dialed a thirteen digit number and waited for the phone to connect. In about ten seconds, he heard the ring tone indicating that the connection was being sought. After two rings, a lady's voice answered.

"Chief teller's office," she said. "How may I help you." (Also in French)

"Would you check my account for a recent deposit?" he asked.

"Certainly, sir. Give me the number please."

Idris repeated a ten digit number for her.

After a pause, she said, "Yes sir, there was a deposit just an hour ago. The amount is Six million French Francs. May I check something else for you, sir?"

"No, thank you. That is all. Have a good day," said Idris and broke the connection. He nodded to Shaheen and they returned to the bunker door in the excavation. When he had brushed off the door where the combination lock was, Idris took out a small notebook from his coat pocket and, using the numbers he had written down some months before, began to rotate the dial, first in one direction and then in another. His first attempt failed, which is not unexpected for the circumstances of a four number code, input in the depth of night with an unsteady hand, but on his second try, the combination worked and he turned the handle to unlatch the door. Once it was unlatched and cracked open a bit, he waved the diggers over to help pull the door fully open and get the rest of the sand out of the way. Idris and Shaheen then took large flashlights and went into the bunker. Both sides of the center aisle were lined with stainless steel cylinders and large artillery shells. There were hundreds. There was a faint aroma of a foreign smell in the bunker, further adding tension to their task. Idris and Shaheen agreed on thirty cylinders and directed the men to begin loading them into the truck.

In about half an hour, they crew had loaded the last cylinders and Shaheen and Idris followed them out the door. Idris carefully closed the door, turned the handle to engage the large cylindrical latches in the perimeter of the door and spun the combination wheel. Then he signaled to the men to throw enough sand back into their excavation to cover the door.

When the door had been sufficiently concealed, they went back to the SUV and the truck and, using the GPS for navigation, began the long trip back to Tripoli. The first streaks of dawn were lighting up the eastern sky when they pulled into Tripoli. About halfway through the city, the SUV turned on to a wide street and the truck kept going straight ahead. It traversed the city from south to north and approached the harbor in due time.

Without hesitation, the truck entered a large door in the side of a docked freighter tied up at the wharf. A set of planks had been placed carefully just a few minutes before to ease the truck into the hold of the ship. As soon as the truck rolled in, the crew set about closing the large door. Before they had finished, the starboard screw began to slowly turn and the ship eased away from the wharf. In twenty minutes, it crossed through the breakwater and into the open ocean. In forty minutes, it was over the horizon.

Rather than go through the Suez canal where the freighter might be boarded and inspected by the British who operated the canal under a treaty, the freighter sailed west and exited the Mediterranean at Gibraltar. It took the freighter eighteen days from there to sail to Karachi.

"Admiral, we need to get eyes on that hangar, any assets of yours in the area?" asked General Behm, the Director of NSA.

"We are working on it, General. I will let you know as soon as we get someone on it," said Admiral Staker. "I am confident that the subject aircraft is the only one in the hangar at present. Whatever comes out will be our target. We need to find out what livery it is painted in and its ID number. This could get really dicey."

"I agree, Admiral," he said. "The air traffic control tapes reveal that a Fed Ex 747 freighter landed about an hour ago and was told to taxi to the Isfahani hangar. I think this aircraft is indeed our mystery aircraft, flying with a faked flight plan. Since it landed at night, but when the airport people were busy, no one probably noticed that it was a

777 and not a 747. I will keep you current as best I can. Thanks for your help."

The President said: "We have to keep this operation completely quiet. If the Russians get wind of it, they may do something rash. If they are involved, they clearly know already what is happening and what the plan is. If we contact them, then they will know that we know there is something afoot and can change plans. As of now, we are not notifying any of our allies, including Israel. This is a serious issue, since we know that they will probably be a target. We will bring them on board as soon as we can, though."

Admiral Staker asked General Mandrake: "Do you guys have any eyes on this hangar? We really need some real time observation."

"No," said Mandrake. "We need to get a drone over there at least for a fly by."

"If you guys can get a drone fly by, can we get the feed, too?" asked Staker.

"Sure," said Mandrake, "Let me see what I can put together. I will get back with you on this secure line."

"Okay, thanks," said Staker and hung up.

Speaking to one of the technicians near him, Staker said: "Griswold, get in touch with our drone people. See what assets we have in the proximity of Karachi. First priority."

"Yes sir," said Griswold,and turned to his computer screen for information.
"Harley, this is Dave, in the tank. What units in the vicinity of Karachi have small drones available? The boss wants this information chop chop."

"I'll get back to you quick. Thanks," said Harley.

In a couple of minutes, the secure phone rang on Staker's desk.

"Sir, this is Harley in the High Altitude Observation Laboratory, next door."

"Yes, Harley. Go ahead," said Staker.

"Sir, we have a recon squad with some of the newer small low speed low altitude drones with television capability on the Nimitz which is presently in the Mediterranean about two hundred miles west of Tel Aviv. They are on alert like all of our units in the Med and Arabian Sea."

"Fine," said Staker. "Ask them how quickly they could deploy a squad with several drones to a position about fifty miles south of Karachi, at sea. Let me hear from you as soon as they answer."

"Yes sir," said Harley and hung up. He looked up at a map of the Karachi area since it was the only feed available.

The phone rang again.
"Sir, this is Harley again. The drone unit advises they can be ready to deploy in half an hour. How will they be transported?"

"Contact the CIC on the Nimitz. Use my name for Authority. Ask them what transportation assets they have. Tell the officer in charge that this is urgent. Report to me with his answer."

"Yes, sir," said Harley and rung off.

"The satellite secure phone rang in the CIC of the Nimitz. The corpsman who answered, held his hand over the phone and spoke to the Captain.

"Sir, it is a man named Harley, calling for Admiral Staker, asking for the officer in charge."

Captain Turnage nodded to the seaman and took the phone.
"This is Captain Turnage, commanding officer of the Nimitz. How can I help you?"

"Sir this is Harley Burger at the CIA Alert Center. Admiral Staker asked me to call you to see if you could rapidly transport our aerial observation squad from the Nimitz to a position fifty nautical south of Karachi, and if so, when could you do that?"

Captain Turnage said: "Give my respects to the Admiral. Tell him that we can launch a COD with the squad on board within half an hour. While they are enroute, ask Admiral Staker where he wants us to land, and get back to me, so I can advise the pilots enroute."

"I will give the Admiral your respects, Captain. Thank you. Admiral Staker confirms that you are to launch the squad as you propose. Email orders to follow."

"Very well," said Turnage and hung up.

Turnage spoke to his Exec, standing nearby.

"Have Blackmire get a COD ready for a maximum range one way hop. Urgent. Advise the Aerial Observation Squad that their transport will be available immediately. Facilitate getting the two groups together. Advise the Air Boss we will need a CAT shot for a COD forthwith."

"Yes, sir," said the Exec, Commander Furlong, and walked immediately to his own phone.

More than a hundred men quickly began to get the squad ready, get them to the COD and get the COD airborne. The fueling crew filled the COD tanks to the top. All windows were cleaned. The aircraft was towed to a ready position on the flight deck. The start cart was connected. In ten minutes, the two pilots, McGee and Bolio, came from the ready room and walked quickly to the COD. Lights on the deck illuminated the aircraft. Men from different auxiliary squads did their thing with the plane getting it ready for a night CAT shot off the Nimitz. The air traffic control officer of the day, called up to the Air Boss' post.

"Chief, we will need a CAT shot to get that COD airborne. The passengers should be boarding as we speak. As soon as the pilot reports ready, you may clear them for departure."

(Note: A CAT shot is the use of a steam powered catapult which is below the flight deck of the carrier. It can propel a fully loaded Carrier On Board aircraft from zero to one hundred twenty five miles per hour in a distance of one hundred forty feet. A night cat shot is especially harrowing, because it is essentially a zero visibility instrument flight rules takeoff because the pilots have no visual references and must rely on their instruments for guidance.)

"Got it, sir," said the Air Boss.

Lieutenant McGee called air traffic control for his clearance.

Air Traffic control told McGee: "You will depart on an initial heading of one zero zero degrees, and expect one zero, ten thousand feet in ten minutes, squawk code will be two two six six. Hand off to Ovda Approach on one two five decimal seven.

Destination to be communicated later. Weather is ceiling three thousand broken, visibility six, haze, pressure is two niner niner eight, wind is from two eight zero at ten knots. Have a good flight."

"Thanks," said McGee and gave a hand signal to the line man standing by the start cart. He hit the overhead switch to start the starboard engine, number two. The rotating beacon began to sweep the deck with its red light. McGee and Bolio went through the pre-flight check list. When they were finished, they confirmed that the temperatures were in the range to permit the takeoff.

McGee keyed the mike button on his yoke.

"Boss, Six one seven is ready to go on CAT Two."

McGee keyed the intercom and told Lieutenant Felson to have his crew brace for the CAT shot.

"Six one seven, you are cleared for the CAT shot. Have a safe flight."

"Roger, six one seven understands cleared for the CAT shot. Thanks."

The yellow clad deck hand raised his right arm and whirled it to signal the pilot to apply full power. When the gauges indicated full power, Lieutenant McGee gave a thumbs up to the deck hand and saluted.

The deck hand knelt and put his hand on the deck. The CAT operator, who was watching from his secure position just below deck, pushed the red button with a large number two on it. There was a rush of steam and a loud pulse of mechanical noise as the COD was propelled down the deck. One hundred forty feet later, it crossed over the end of the deck and vaulted into the black night.

Chapter 11

Jefe had just sat down in the canvas chair on the patio. He took a large towel and dried himself. The temperature of the sea water, the outside shower and the sunlit deck seemed the same. It was delicious. He turned to watch his long time friend Alita shower off the sand from the beach and the salt water at the corner of the veranda next to the house. He was so glad that the builder put an outside shower there, so they could get the sand off of themselves outside of the house. She turned her face into the spray from the shower and the water flowed over her face and head, bringing every strand of her black hair into a close knit cap, like an otter, he thought. He marveled at how good she looked with a nice tan against her white two piece swim suit. They had been lovers for more than twenty years. Both during and after their marriages to others. Her husband, Bernie was in an assisted living facility in Cornwall, and would probably never recover his ability to speak, walk or feed himself after a terrible stroke. He had been there for two years.

Jefe and his wife, Gwen, had decided to part company amicably eight years ago. She had suffered enough, he thought. His long absences and the constant danger of the line of work he was in was too much to ask of a wife, he thought. She finally agreed with him, and moved out. These days, she was having a fine time in a retirement community in Scottsdale.

Jefe marveled at how youthful Alita looked as she ambled toward him in the Greek sunlight. He had owned this villa on Keros for fifteen years and the live-in caretaker he found took care of it when he was off on "projects." Andrea was a very overweight, dark haired Greek woman who was perfectly happy to maintain the place and stay out of Jefe's way when he was there. She would fix meals and leave them on the dining room table. She would ring a small bell to tell him that food was ready and then she would disappear to tend to another chore. It was a delightful arrangement for them both. Andrea's children and grandchildren could visit when he was going to be gone for a while, and he would always alert her when he was on his way, so they could clean up the place, stock the wine cellar and refrigerator and get out of the way.

Jefe and Alita cherished the privacy that their villa provided. It was "a world away." He kept an ancient Volkswagen beetle for the few times they needed to go into town and stock up the food and drink or to go to the magnificent seaside restaurant for a dinner and to enjoy a golden sunset over the harbor.

He poured them both a small glass of Pinot Grigio and handed hers to Alita. She clinked her glass against his and smiled as she glided into her seat.

Just as she relaxed into her seat, they both heard the tiny bell indicating that Andrea had put their lunch on the table. He waved to Alita to stay in her seat and he toddled off to get their tray and bring it to their glass topped table on the veranda.

As he walked to the double doors that led to the dining room off of the veranda, he could see up the coast several miles. It was a beautiful sight. He smiled with gratitude. The view in the other direction was blocked by a large outcrop of limestone that bled large white bands down its steep slope. Perhaps many would have rejected this villa because of the one way view, but Jefe liked it right away and grabbed it up when he got the chance.

He and Alita had been there by arrangement for about two weeks. They had flown in separately to Piraeus and taken the sea taxi to the island. The villa had its own water well and electric generator. Jefe had had to buy a new one shortly after he bought the villa and the new one was quieter and more economical. He had installed solar panels on the roof where they could not be seen from the deck and that helped store up electricity in twelve volt batteries which were used to light the house and run the refrigerator. There was no need for air conditioning, so there was plenty of electrical capacity with the panels and the generator. With a propane stove and furnace, the villa was pretty much independent of utilities.

"I love the sunlight here, don't you?" Alita asked Jefe. (By the way, she knew him by his real name and did not even know that he used the nom de guerre of "Jefe" when he was working for Mr. Murfree. She had her own pet name for him anyway. (Your security clearance is not near high enough to know Jefe's real name, so just get over it.) Jefe had told her that he worked for Mr. Murfree, but he did not tell her who Mr. Murfree was. She thought he was some kind of consultant to a large multi-national corporation. Someday soon, Jefe hoped to take her to meet Mr. Murfree when they swung through the eastern U.S.)

"Yes, it is softer here than elsewhere, I think, but maybe it is just the company."

He took a small plate and put three raw oysters on it for her with a dollop of horse radish sauce and a small silver fork, and when he turned around to hand it to her, she had stood up and said, "This wet swim suit is such an irritant when I am trying to get dry. You don't mind it if I change, do you?" she asked.

Without waiting for his reply, she unfastened the top and shrugged out of it. "Goodness she is such a beautiful woman," he thought. Before he could speak, she forked her thumbs inside of each side of the bottom of her white two piece suit and gracefully dropped it to the flagstones. She then, with a smirk of satisfaction at the lack of the restriction she slid back into her canvas chair and gave him a beaming smile. With her right hand, she reached out and took the small plate with the oysters from his hand.

For a moment, he was speechless. Then he said: "You make me so grateful," he said. "You are so much woman. I am smitten each time you do that. Will you promise to do that as long as we live?" he asked.

"Because you appreciate it so much, of course, I will," she said.

Out of the corner of his hearing, he heard the tiny tinkle of Andrea's bell. He looked toward the double doors. She had put a small table outside the doors and on it sat Jefe's satellite telephone.

He got up and walked slowly across the flagstones to the phone.

"Hello," he said.

"Please hold for Mr. Murfree," said the voice on the other end.

In a few moments, the familiar voice of the President came on.

"Say the word," he said.

Jefe said "Tupelo."

Now both he and the President knew that they were talking to the right person.

"I need to alert you that we believe that terrorists have hijacked that Malaysian airliner. We think they are headed to Karachi with it. We also suspect that a Chechen sympathizing KGB Colonel and some others stole three medium yield nuclear weapons Thursday night from a warehouse in Chechnya and are flying or trucking them to Karachi. I awakened Lero and Jean and I have them on a B-1 over the Pacific on their way to Mumbai at high speed. I have appointed Lero as point man on this project. He and Jean are to reconnoiter the hangar at Karachi, but I need you to get them a local person to help them. We have a Naval Reconnaissance team with small drones on a fishing boat just off the coast south of Karachi, but their effectiveness is in doubt. Lero and Jean will arrive in Karachi from Mumbai on an Air India flight in about four hours. Call me back as soon as you line somebody up to meet them and help them. They will also need weapons, breaching gear, appropriate flash bang grenades and the like to storm the cockpit if they can indeed get on board, dark suits, food, night vision goggles and anything else you can think of that they can carry in a suitcase. I hope they can talk their way into the hangar under the pretext of being there to pick up a business jet being serviced for an Emirati sheik. Call me as soon as you can, Jefe."

"Will do, sir. Alita and I are on Keros. I can leave on short notice if you need me to."

"Thanks, my friend. Right now, I just need your organizational skills and contacts. Talk to you soon." He rang off.

Jefe held the phone in his hand without putting it down as when ending a normal call.

Alita could see that and walked over to him. My, she was gorgeous in the Greek sunlight. The way she undulated was captivating. "More about that later," he thought.

She could tell that something was up. She asked: "Is there trouble?"

"That was the boss. I need to make a few calls to set up a meeting. I better do that in my office. Stay here and enjoy the oysters and the sunshine. I will be back in a few minutes."

While he was telling her this, she kept drawing closer to him. She reached up and kissed him lightly just like he liked and nodded her understanding.

He could not help watching her walk back to her chair. Business is business, and this was urgent, but he thought the President would not begrudge him five seconds to watch the naked love of his life walk to her chair.

In a few seconds, he tore his gaze from her and turned and went into the double doors. The villa had a full basement hewn out of the native limestone. The contractor who built the villa had installed a tile floor in the basement to even up the floor and make it smooth. He had placed a nice oriental rug over the tiles to make it comfortable to work in bare feet. His office was in the corner of one of the two rooms in the lower floor. He slid into his desk chair and dialed the satellite phone.

Chapter 12

In about half a minute, after three rings, a sleepy voice answered in Urdu: "Amahl Taxicab Company."

Jefe asked, "May I speak to Rangit please?" in Urdu.

"Yes, this is he," said the sleepy voice.

"Rangit, this is Jefe. I need you to do something for me. Are you able to give me some time?"

"Sure, Jefe," said Rangit, his voice shook off the drowsiness and picked up a little excitement.

"I have two passengers arriving on Air India flight One Fifty Five in approximately three hours. They are in need of transport and your assistance, as well as some equipment. They may need to breach an airplane flight deck. Are you in a position to supply a couple of assault rifles, pistols, some thermite charges, night vision goggles, some flash bang grenades, some nylon rope, some dark colored suits and hoods, flashlights, two hand held radio transmitters, an assault pharmaceutical package, some military food rations and drinks for a few days, and other boarding party equipment?"

"Yes, at the Safe House we have anything like that they might need. How big are these people?"

"The man is about five ten, one hundred sixty five pounds, and fit. The lady is about five feet four and weighs about one hundred five pounds. His shoe size is ten, hers is six. Can you get all that equipment packed into a couple of duffel bags and in your taxicab and meet them at their plane when it lands?"

"Two hours is enough time, my friend. How will I recognize them?"

"The lady will be carrying a red purse. They will be traveling in the name of Mr. and Mrs. Dan Roman. I will tell them that they can expect to encounter you at the baggage carousel. Is that alright?"

"It is fine. I will call you to confirm that I am at the airport and ready."

"Thanks, Rangit. Hope to see you soon."

He rang off.

Jefe went back up to the veranda but took his satellite phone with him. He found that Alita had lay down on the king sized velour covered air mattress to take some sun. He dropped his bathing suit and joined her.

Rangit got up out of the red leather overstuffed chair that was his refuge when he was waiting for a call. He had "appropriated" it from a government office several years prior when there was a "change in government." The Mercedes taxicab was beginning to show its years, but since he maintained it well, it would last for many more. He slid behind the wheel and motored off toward the waterfront.

Using the door opener he kept in the glove box, he pushed the button in front of a large green wooden door in a grimy inset in the wall of an old warehouse. The door silently slid aside and he drove in quickly. As soon as he was inside, he hit the button again to close the door. When it closed, he was completely in the dark. He fished out his flashlight from the door pocket and lit it to show his way to the switches for the interior lights. Even though he did not know the exact number, Rangit was one of eight "assets" who had a door opener for this warehouse. Inside the room he had pulled his taxicab into was about thirty feet long and about twenty feet wide, solid concrete floor, brick walls, no paint. He went to the switches on the side wall and turned on the lights. In the back of the warehouse, was a doorway. The door was massive oak with a large keyhole on the left side. He turned his key in the lock and pushed the door open. Inside, in rows of boxes and cabinets, were the items he needed. He opened a wooden box in the left row and got out two Heckler and Koch MP5 nine millimeter assault weapons. He put them on the bench to the side and made a note in his notebook for inventory replenishment. Then he went over to the ammunition box where he retrieved an ammunition can of Israeli Military Industries nine millimeter ammunition. After each item, he noted what and how many he took so the quartermaster of the "group" could restock the inventory. Next he filled three thirty round magazines for each weapon and put a hundred rounds of the ammunition, loose, in a small canvas bag. He got two Beretta X4 pistols from the black cabinet next to the wooden crate, each with four magazines which he filled from the ammunition can. Then he went to the metal foot locker by the right wall and retrieved two sets of night vision goggles, boarding party Randall type knives with scabbards, and a set of man's running shoes, black, size ten. For her he chose a similar pair, but size six. In a cabinet on the wall, hung about twenty coverall type light weight "Ninja" style outfits. He chose one for a man about five ten and one for a shorter person and threw them over his arm. By this time, he had accumulated enough gear to begin filling the two black ballistic nylon duffel bags he had put on the table. He put all the gear in that he had already chosen, then went to the food locker at the rear of the room. He got four MREs and six one liter bottles of G2 Gatorade for each of them and returned them to the duffels. The duffels were beginning to fill up.

Next he went to the locker beside the clothes locker and opened its double doors. He chose four boxes from the left side that were about five by five inches on the ends and twelve inches long. Each contained a thermite charge with adhesive attachment pads. Once ignited, these would quietly burn a foot wide hole in any door, metal or otherwise. Beside those boxes, he retrieved eight flash bang grenades and four tear gas grenades and a pair of light weight Israeli gas masks. Now the duffels were beginning to really fill up. He remembered to get a pair of black cotton socks for each person from the footlocker, too. A pair of black leather gloves for each went in, too. He got four flashlights from the right side of the cabinet. One large and one small for each of them.

Now things were really coming together. He stood for a moment, just looking down into the duffels and thinking. Satisfied that he had equipped each bag with what was needed, he zipped them shut and lugged each to the trunk of the taxicab. As a last detail, he went to a small notebook on the back desk and made a cryptic entry: "Number four visited on Tuesday, the fifth at twenty hundred hours. Equipment taken. Need to restock, " and he left his hand written list of what he had taken.

Then, he returned to the switches on the side wall of the main room, turned them off and used the flashlight to make his way to the taxicab. He opened the door and closed it after exiting the same way he had entered. The taxi pulled slowly out of the narrow alley and into night.

In twenty minutes, he was at the taxi stand at Jinnah Airport, waiting. He dialed his satellite phone from inside the cab where the tinted windows gave him some concealment.

"Hello," said Jefe.

"All is ready. Waiting at the airport," said Rangit.

"Thanks, be careful." Rangit put the satellite phone in the glove box and retrieved his favorite carry pistol, an old Radom nine millimeter. Now, he could pretend to take a nap as he waited for his fares.

Chapter 13

"Hello," said the aide on duty.

"Tell Mr. Murfree that Jefe called. Message is 'Agent is in place, ready for arrivals.'"

"Thank you," said the aide and pressed the button to end the call.

The President called his National Security Advisor, Mark Werth, on his desk phone.
"Mark, do you have your people analyzing the various possible scenarios on this aircraft?

"Yes, Mr. President. We have called everyone in. I have assigned a lead person for each theory we presently have and I have a group just tasked with coming up with new theories of what they will do with that plane. Do you want me to come in and brief you on the situation at present?"

"Sure, Mark. I don't want to get too deep into all of the possibilities, but I would appreciate some time to compare thoughts with you. I will meet you in my study in ten minutes if that is OK."

"I can be there, Mr. President. See you then."

The President strode down from the residence to the oval office complex and got to his study just a minute or so before Mark arrived. The President always wore a coat and tie when he was in the Oval Office complex.

"What do you and your guys think?" asked the President.

"Well, sir, all of us agree that there is a high probability that whoever is in charge intends to use that aircraft for some kind of a strike. The vital link is determining who is pulling the strings, so to speak. If it is an Al Qaeda group, with that plane's range and carrying capacity, we think they will try a trans-Atlantic attack on us. We believe that the chance that they will hit Israel is minor, on the order of ten percent. On the other hand, if the Iranians and Hezbollah are in charge, the probability that they will hit Israel is about fifty-fifty, we think. If it is the Chechens, we think it is more probable that they will hit Russia, hoping to get two birds with one stone, so to speak. If they hit Moscow, the primary target will be destroyed and Moscow will most likely believe it was done by us and will retaliate against us. In a way, that is the most dangerous theory we presently entertain. We think that, even though the ISI has the airplane, a strike against Afghanistan on behalf of the Taliban would be foolish, because the Taliban are so interspersed among the Afghans that it would kill as many loyal Afghans as Taliban.

Another scenario that our guys came up with is that the Pakistan nationalists may try a strike against India. We feel that the probability of that is very slight, but cannot be ruled out."

"We don't have any resident assets with the capability of seeing what is going on in that hangar, so we are kinda stymied on that front. Our friends at NSA have re-tasked a satellite to a geosynchronous orbit over the area, but it is twenty two thousand miles high. We cannot use the Space Station for observations on its passes over the area because there are three Russian cosmonauts on board presently. We have the Nimitz, the Reuben James and the Utah converging at best speed on a point about one hundred fifty miles south of Karachi. We have a COD from the Nimitz on it way to the area with an aerial observation team with drones, but we don't know just yet where they can land. That decision must be made in the next hour."

Staker asked Harley:"What kind of assets do we have to land the COD in the Gulf in about three hours?"

"I have been checking that, sir. The Reagan will be in position in another hour and could receive the COD. That would be the best plan. The only other seaborne asset we have is the Harwell, a helicopter carrier about three hundred miles south of Karachi. It does have a trap, though, but if we land the COD there, it will not be able to take off again. It would have to be lifted off by crane and re-positioned to a carrier or onto land."

"Another thing, sir, I talked with the captain of the Harwell. He says that he will have to hover several helicopters when the COD lands to make room for it to trap on the deck. He is fine with that, though."

"Good work, Harley. Notify the captain of the Harwell that we want him to follow that plan. Tell him to steam at flank speed north and advise us of his position every hour. I will have someone notify the COD of the possibility that we will want the COD to land on the Harwell, but let's plan on the Reagan as the primary landing site. Have someone notify the Observation Squad of the plan, and tell the captain that we will want him to provide a helicopter to take the Observation Squad to a smaller boat that can take them to a secure position so they can set up their drone base."

"Will do, sir. Anything else?"

"Yes. Find out if we have a squad of SEALS in the area who can take the Observation Squad to where we decide to place it."

"Will do, sir, and will advise."

Harley rang the Special Ops headquarters in Florida.

"Special Operations Command, Sergeant Grimm, speaking."

"Sergeant Grimm, this is Harley Burger at the CIA Ops Center. Admiral Staker wants to know where the nearest team of SEALs is to the Northern Gulf of Arabia. He wants to know numbers and capability. Do they have inflatable boats with motors?"

"Harley, I will find out and call you back. Is this number OK?"

"Sure is, and Staker says first priority."

"Understood. Will call you right back."

Both hung up.

Grimm relayed the message to Commander Buckmaster, the Officer of the Day.

Grimm called the Operations Center of the Special Operations Command.

"Command Center, Lieutenant Varney speaking."

"Lieutenant Varney, this is Commander Buckmaster. I need to know the nearest SEAL team to the northern Gulf of Arabia. Need to know if they have inflatables with motors. First priority."

"Roger, sir. Will get on this and get you an answer."

Varney keyed his computer keyboard and it displayed the location of all the SEAL teams under their command. The manifest showed that Team Five was on a Guided Missile Frigate passing through the Straits of Hormuz as of the last hourly report. His wall chart showed that the Straits were about five hundred miles south west of Karachi. The communications code for the Harwell was next to the data he was reading. He reached for his secure telephone and keyed in the numbers.

"USS Harwell Operations, Lieutenant Wilcox speaking."

"Lieutenant Wilcox, this is Harley Burger at the CIA Ops Center. We need to know how quickly you could launch Seal Team Five by helicopter for a mission to the north end of the Gulf of Arabia. They are needed at a position just offshore Karachi, at night. First priority."

"Harley, I will consult with the commander of the SEAL team and call you back."

"Thanks," said Harley and broke the connection.

"Admiral, National Reconnaissance Office, Satellite Ops Center, advises that in the last hour, several heavy trucks have arrived at the Ispahani hangar."

"Harley, advise the President and his National Security Advisor that we have made that observation. It looks to me like they are going to

load at least one nuke and some chemical or
biological weapons with all those trucks showing up.
Tell the President and his National Security
Advisory that that is our thinking just now."

"Will do, sir. Thanks."

Chapter 14

When Lero awoke, he was slumped in the seat next to Jean's seat. The flight attendant had been watching to see when he awakened and came over to him.

"Sir, they have been calling to talk to you, but instructed not to wake you. They said when you awoke, to call on the secure link. Are you ready to talk to them?"

Lero stirred some more and by now, Jean was stirring, too.

"Give me a minute to go to the head and then put the call through," he said, and got up to visit the plumbing. As he exited, Jean was coming up the aisle toward him. As they passed each other, they rotated to let themselves pass and she gave him a brief hug.

He took a seat at the small table near the front of the passenger cabin and the flight attendant handed him the headset.

When he said:"Hello," the voice on the other end said: "Hold just a moment, please."

There was a short pause and the voice he

recognized spoke: "Hello, this is Mr. Murfree, say the word."

Lero said: "Houston."

Now they both knew that they were talking to the person intended.

"My people tell me that you are making good time. You are about five hundred miles west of Johnston Island and the planners tell me that there will be an aerial refueling in the next hour. Our plan at this time is to have you land at Mumbai, since it is a very busy commercial airport, your arrival will be masked by lots of traffic and night time. You will transfer to a COD which will take you to the Reagan which will be positioning itself about one hundred fifty miles south of Karachi. Jean will transfer to a P-8 Poseidon and will join in the groups observing what is happening in the Ispahani hangar at Jinnah Airport. Since we last talked the plane has remained in the hangar, but there has been a lot of activity."

"In order to get you up to speed and to let me attend to some other matters, I have asked Admiral Staker to feed all material data and video to you while airborne by scrambled satellite transmissions. You will hear all relevant conversations and be able to participate in them. You will see all maps of deployments, too."

"Right now, it is my belief that you will want to wait to see what direction the plane takes on departure to decide what remedy to use. Give me reports when you are able, but you will be the point man on this operation. The code name is Cherokee. Take advice from Admiral Staker and General Behm at NSA, but you are in charge. Captain Smithers on the Nimitz has been informed of the situation and has been told that you will coordinate this effort from his ship. All of our assets and personnel in the theatre are on alert and ready to do what they can to contribute. At your speed, including the slow down for the refueling, we estimate you will be in Mumbai in five hours. If your mission were not classified, we could claim several speed records. Let me know as soon as you are on the Reagan ready to function from there. I am grateful to you, Lero. Talk to you later."

"Thank you, Mr. President. I will report from the Reagan. Good evening."

When they landed at Mumbai, the B-1 taxied to the north west corner of the field. Parked there were a COD to take Lero to the Reagan and a P-8 Poseidon for Jean to join the el-int team to try to interpret and decipher any electronic information they could. As they walked to the P-8, there was a breeze coming from the ocean. Lero walked Jean up to the steps and stopped to talk to her.

"Be careful with yourself. Remember there is only one of you. We probably won't get to talk during this operation. This is very serious business. I feel a heavy responsibility here. Please pray for me and the other guys when you get a chance. Pray that we do the right thing. You are the high point of my life, Jean. I want to be back with you in Tucson," he said.

She teared up a little and then got hold of herself. She said to him: "The President has high confidence in you and so do I. When this is over we can spend some time catching up on important things. Remember I love you, wherever you go."

The hugged firmly and kissed briefly. Then, she went up the stairs and when she was safely on board, he fast walked to the COD. The pilots had the off side engine running and started the other as he went up the short ladder to his seat. In ten minutes, both aircraft were gone. After refueling, the B-1 left for Diego Garcia.

Lero put on a headset so he could listen to and talk to the pilots. He was strapped into a bucket seat on the right side of the passenger compartment.

"Welcome aboard, sir. We should have you to the Reagan in about an hour. She has been steaming at full speed since yesterday morning and is now about five hundred miles south south east of Karachi."

"Thanks, fellows. I appreciate the ride. I would like to come forward and watch your landing if I might. A night trap in a COD is a real adventure, I understand."

"We will call you when we get close. You will have to strap in in one of the jump seats behind us for the landing, though."

"Thanks, just give me a call," said Lero and tried to nap for a few minutes.

"Sir, hate to wake you, but there is a call from Jefe on the scrambler. We will connect you."

"OK," said Lero.

In a few seconds, Jefe came on. "Say the word," he said.

"Houston," said Lero, and they both knew they were talking to the right person.

"This is just a detail, but we have found out that the largest nuke that the Pakistanis have is rated at fifty kilotons, about the size of the Hiroshima bomb. A bomb that size would be devastating to the Israelis if it were dropped on Tel Aviv. The reason that Israel remains a credible target based on that is that these guys could bomb Tel Aviv and devastate it and thirty miles of so around it, and leave Gaza and most of the West Bank undamaged. They also would not want to damage Jerusalem, you know, because that is where the Dome of the Rock temple is where Mohammed is supposed to have ascended to Heaven. It is ironic that Jerusalem is sacred to three major religions. In this case, it gives each a reason not to destroy it."

"Thanks, I agree with your analysis. However, what if they choose to load more than one bomb on the plane?" asked Lero.

"We need to give that some thought," said Jefe.

"Right now, with skimpy information about who is involved, we must include in the possibilities that whoever is in charge intends to use this aircraft to strike the United States. We are theorizing that they will load it with a couple of nukes and use the rest of the carrying capacity for chemical weapons and biological weapons. Our analysts theorize, in one scenario, that they will disguise this plane as one from another airline, and somehow try to sneak into the U.S. as a regularly scheduled flight. Most of the critical areas in the eastern U.S. are reachable with this plane's range. This is scary."

"Sir, if they try a strike across the Atlantic, we will have several hours to deal with the threat before it gets close enough to the coast to do any damage. I agree that your guys have a good theory. We just need to get some more intel on what is going on in that hangar. What is the status of the Aerial Observation Squad?"

"They are helicopter bound at present, expected to land on the Reuben James within the next thirty minutes."

"With the range of the drones they have, we should be in a position to launch the first flight within the hour, then," said Lero.

"Right," said Jefe. "If they can fly by the hangar at low altitude, we should be able to get some video shortly. We noticed several heavy trucks left the hangar under cover of darkness and several more arrived. If we can get a peek at the personnel in the hangar, we may be in a better position to guess their plan."

"I agree. I will call you as soon as I get set up on the Reagan. Jean is on the P-8 which will be patrolling south off the coast."

"Good enough," said Jefe. "Don't worry about her, please. We have high cover watching over that airplane."

"I have high confidence in our people, sir, but I just am concerned, as you can understand."

"I do understand. You and she are like my children to me. Her pop and I were close friends."

"Thank you, sir. I appreciate your watching out for us. Call you from the Reagan."

"Niner two four, you are fifty DME. Begin descent to one zero, ten thousand feet, please. Report reaching."

"Niner two four, roger."

Lero felt an immediate, but smooth reduction in power and pitch as the COD began its descent. The wind noise did not change."

"Chief, we have a COD inbound, ETA fifteen minutes."

"Roger, we will be ready for him."

"Trap officer, set resistance for a COD, ETA fourteen minutes."

"Roger, Boss. We are set for him."

"Captain, we expect the COD in thirteen minutes. All deck personnel are ready and the trap is adjusted for him."

"Thanks, Murf. Advise when they land."

"Roger, sir, will do."

Chapter 15

Chief Grinstead said to Lero: "Sir, there is a call for you on the scrambler from the P-8."

"OK, Chief," Lero said and took the handset.

"This is Lero," he said.

"This is Jean. Say the words," said Jean.

"Canadian Sunset," said Lero. "Say the words."

"Desert darling," she said. Now they knew they were sure whom they were talking to.

"Sorry to intrude, but my scanner is picking up a transmission from the Reagan that is on a frequency that is not on their normal list of frequencies. It is voice, simplex, and in the clear. What concerns me, in addition, is that it is in Urdu. We have recorded all we have intercepted, and our intel guys are translating it now. We transmitted our recordings to the NSA at Fort Meade. I think you may have a mole on the Reagan. If your security people have a direction finder, they can find this guy when he is transmitting. I can call when he transmits and your guys can turn on their DF and track him down. This is scary. Just to think you have a mole on the Reagan, of all times."

Lero said, "Yes, our security people have DF capability. I will assign a crew to it and if you will let me know when you are receiving any broadcast, I will alert them and we will see if we can catch this guy. Great work. I miss you."

"I miss you, too," said Jean. "Call you later."

Lero thought to himself: "Urdu is the fourth most popular language on earth, after Mandarin Chinese, English and Spanish. This guy could be from anywhere in a vast area of Asia. Under these circumstances, most likely Pakistani, but could be Indian or Afghan, too."

Lero walked quickly over to where Captain Warshovsky was conferring with another officer. The Captain saw Lero walk up and recognized some urgency in his expression.

"Sir, I need to speak with you securely," said Lero.

"Come with me, said the Captain, without hesitation.

He led Lero down a passageway to a compartment off of the companionway. He opened the door with an electronic key. He reached in and turned on the light and motioned for Lero to go in ahead of him. When they were both in the small deeply padded room, he turned to Lero and said: "What's up?"

"Jean just called from the P-8. They are picking up intermittent broadcasts from this ship in Urdu. She thinks we may have a mole on board. No one else knows what I am telling you except Jean."

"Let me get my G-2 (Chief of Intelligence) on this right away. Be careful, of course, whatever you say about anything in front or within earshot of any sailor until we get this dealt with. I don't intend to tell anyone but my G-2 about this for now, OK?"

"Sure," said Lero, and they left the room. Lero went to his compartment to lie down for a while.

Warshovsky went back to the CIC (Combat Information Center) and found Commander Burns, his G-2. Then he took Burns to the secure room and filled him in. When they came out of the secure room, Burns went one way and the Captain went another.

Burns summoned Chief Petty Officer Peterson from the Avionics Shop on the Flight Deck. When Peterson reported, Burns took him to the secure room.

"Chief, the P-8 above has reported that we have intermittent broadcasts from this ship in Urdu. We obviously have a mole on board. This is very touchy. I want you to pick a small group, maybe two men and get them on this right away. Check every antenna on board for a splitter and trace it back if you can. I will determine what frequency he is using and you can keep a hand held transceiver set to that frequency to help you trace this guy. When you have leads, report to me in person. Do not transmit or use the phones on board to talk with me about this. If anyone give you any trouble, report them to me immediately. On board, only you and I and the captain know about this. Keep it quiet. Any questions?"

"No, sir. I will get two of my best men on this right away. Where is your compartment in case I need to see you when you are off duty?"

"I am in compartment E343 on the second deck."

Peterson saluted and went hurriedly back to the Avionics Shop.

Burns got Lero to call Jean on the P-8.

After they said "the words," Lero asked Jean what frequency the mole was transmitting on. She said one thirty six point seven two five, near the top of the aviation VHF band. Lero said, "Thanks, but we need to continue to scan on all of the aviation band in case he is using other frequencies in some sort of a rotation. Your discovery may prove to be crucially important. I am so proud of the scanner you developed. Keep up the good work. Are you able to get some rest?"

"Yes," she said. We have enough fuel for fifteen hours on board. I take a nap when I need to. The scanner has a recorder on it, so I won't miss anything, but I miss you, my man."

"I miss you, too," he said. "Talk to you later."

"OK, Bye," she said.

"This guy is no Italian. He is a Palestinian. Thanks to the Israelis, who take a retinal scan of all the prisoners they process, this guy showed up. He was captured north of the Israeli-Lebanese border two years ago during the Hezbollah attacks. The Israelis traded him and ninety nine others for one of their soldiers that the Palestinians had captured about eighteen months ago. We are working on it, but we think presently that the Palestinians captured an American sailor during shore leave in Pireaus a couple of years ago and substituted this guy for him. He looks enough like the Italian they captured that the subterfuge worked. He has been sending information to someone, we still don't know whom, for several months. He put a splitter on one of our VHF antennas and led the wires into a closet off of the flight deck. Chief Peterson and his guy, Bemos, found the lead. They caught this guy about an hour ago, red handed, using a hand held transceiver connected to the lead. What should we do with him, sir?"

Commander Burns said: "Keep him in the brig for now. I will notify our interrogators to visit him. Unless we get a report of any more transmissions, let's just lay low for now. I will let you know if we need you again. Nice work, Chief."

"Thanks, sir," said Peterson, with a snappy salute.

In an hour or so, Peterson came back to see Burns. "Sir," I think it would be a good idea if we would use this guy's rig to send bogus messages to whoever is on the other end. There is an Urdu speaker on the P-8 and we can use him to imitate this guy. If you will give me permission, I will contact the P-8 and get someone on this. We might just disrupt them a bit before they detect the ruse."

"Good thinking, Peterson. That is a good idea. Contact the P-8 as you propose. Use my name and reference the Reagan for approval. Let me know what they say and what they propose to do, please."

"Will do, sir," said Peterson and hurried to the console.

Chapter 16

"We are ready to leave with the trucks now, Major," said Captain Shahreza.

"Good. Sail at least five hundred nautical miles off shore before you dispose of the bodies. Make sure that each body is carefully and sufficiently weighted. Incinerate all of the baggage after searching it for valuables. Keep any currency you find. Melt any gold jewelry so that we will not run the chance that it will fall into the wrong hands and be recognized. Incinerate anything that might be recognized. Take your time. After you dump the bodies and take care of the baggage, sail on southerly for several days, then turn around and come back to port. No radio contact with us. Contact only maritime authorities for clearances to dock when you are inbound. Be very thorough. If all goes well, divide the currency with your crew as a bonus. Tell them to forget what they saw. Tell them it could be hazardous to their health if any of them ever speaks about the mission."

Captain Shahreza said: "We will do as you order, sir. We are leaving now."

"Very well," said Major Gilan and returned the salute.

It was the middle of the night when the hangar doors parted just enough to let the trucks out. They wove their way down to the harbor and completed loading the cargo onto the ship that awaited without delay. By dawn, the ship was a hundred nautical miles off shore.

Chapter 17

"Dimitri, what have you found out about that damned airplane?" asked Admiral Koshenko.

"We don't have any further information, Admiral," said Captain Sergeivitch.

"It is most strange and suspicious that the aircraft would cease to transmit with its transponder and that the ACARS system would be turned off just after the plane was handed off to Ho Chi Minh Radar. It makes it much more likely that this is no accident. Of course, there is always the possibility that it was an accident, that there was a catastrophic decompression shortly after they reached their cruising altitude of thirty five thousand feet, but even if it were an accident, the crew would have had time to transmit a Mayday or switch the transponder to the emergency code after the crew donned their oxygen masks. The suddenness and totality of loss of radio contact is most suspicious. Is our asset at Boeing reporting anything?"

"No, sir, we have not heard from her. I will report to you immediately if we receive any information from her."

"If this aircraft has been seized by terrorists, we may not be able to discern their intent until they strike. If the plane is indeed on the ground somewhere in the hands of terrorists, they could have any one of many intended targets, depending on the make-up of the terrorist group. We believe if the plane is held by some group associated with Al Qaeda, they may try a trans-Atlantic strike at the United States. If the holders of the plane are associated with Iran and Hezbollah, they may try to strike Israel. The irony of such a strike is that millions of Palestinians would be killed, too. Frankly, the group that frightens me the most is the Chechens. They are so hot headed and reckless, they might just try to hit Moscow."

"There are many theories, Admiral. One of our best analysts believes that we need to consider that it is a Pakistani Nationalist group and that they plan to hit India. There is no love lost between Pakistan and India and if the Indians are unable to discern the source of the attack, they might just retaliate against Pakistan with nuclear weapons."

"That brings in another facet of this problem, Yuri," said Admiral Koshenko. "What if the plane is filled with chemical or biological weapons, or both? The target country would have to take remedial steps as well as mount a counter attack against the perceived perpetrators. They could get it wrong and set off a nuclear war between parties who had nothing to do with the attack."

"All we can do is our best, sir. I will report to you any relevant information as soon as received. Do you intend to stay here in your Kremlin office while this plays out?"

"Yes, Yuri. Minutes might make the difference. I will use my quarters here until this thing is secure."

Chapter 18

"Simpson, come and look at this," said Thomas Redwine, the night supervisor of the ACARS station in Singapore. Our geosynchronous satellite is over a point south of the peninsula of India. It has been receiving ping messages from the suspected aircraft for four hours now. Since the Malaysian Air people did not subscribe to the full ACARS program, the report is only whether the engines are running or not. Since there are no other stations within range, we cannot triangulate the signals back from the aircraft, but can only tell how far the signal is from the satellite by Doppler analysis."

"What is it telling you now, Rudy?" asked Simpson.

"Well, sir, the distance from the satellite is easily determined by our calculating software. The problem is that the plane could be on a track southerly from the last point of contact or it could be going northwesterly. Until we get info from some other receiving station, it could be either path. Now that the pings have stopped, we may never get any data from another receiving station."

"Have you plotted the tracks that the plane could have taken?" asked Simpson.

"Yes. The Malaysian authorities are reporting that the plane took the southerly route and they are ignoring the possible northwesterly route."

"We cannot afford to ignore that northwesterly possibility. Has someone reported this information to the NSA or CIA?"

"No, sir. Only the technicians you can see here in this room and you and I know this."

"OK, then I will report it."

Simpson picked up his phone and dialed a number he retrieved from a small note book in his desk drawer.

"Ops Center, Hunt speaking."

"Mr. Hunt, this is Elroy Simpson at the ACARS receiving station in Singapore. We want to report to you that our satellite, which is probably the only station that has received any pings from the missing flight from Kuala Lumpur, is producing data that indicate that it is just as likely that the missing airplane took a northwesterly heading as that it took a southerly heading."

"This is being recorded, Mr. Simpson. Thank you very much. I will forward this information to our Watch Officer. May he call you back at this number?"

"Yes," said Simpson. "We will be here for three more hours on this shift and someone will replace me. I will brief him on the situation and your or your men may call us at any time."

"Thank you, Mr. Simpson. Good evening."

Chapter 19

Lord Cosby was watching his teen aged son practice with his polo team with a newly acquired horse. The teams were trying to teach the younger members how to bunch up to press the other team toward the goal. All those beautiful horses and skilled riders were an inspiring sight. The earth shook when they roared past. On the bank about twenty yards from the field boundary, he could feel the hoof beats and it increased the thrill of competition.

Inside his shirt pocket, his cell phone vibrated. He retrieved it and answered.

"Cosby," he spoke.

"Sir, this is Morford at the Ops Center. Could you come in? We have a situation."

"Of course. I will be there in twenty minutes. Thank you."

Cosby knew that the officer would give no clue as to the type of problem because he had trained his men to do just that. He also knew that they would not call him in over a minor flap. This had to be something important.

He walked the few feet to where his wife was attentively watching the practice and told her he had to go. She could tell from his expression that it was necessary.

"I will get a cab. I will leave the car with James to bring you home," he said. He kissed her sweetly behind her left ear and turned and walked the hundred yards to the parking area. There were several taxicabs waiting since it was near the end of the practice session and the cabbies knew it was a good prospect.

As he entered the taxi, he told the driver: "Waterloo Station, please." That way, anybody overhearing his instruction would not know where he really was going. In about a block, he said to the driver: "Change of plan. Take me to 1213 Stuyvesant Street, please." The cabbie nodded and motored on.

When the taxi pulled up to the front of the ten story office building, Lord Cosby had the fare ready, along with an appropriate gratuity.

"Thank you, sir. Have a good day," the cabbie said as he let Cosby out.

The lobby was small for such a large building. There was a wall ahead of him with double doors leading to the offices on the first floor. The lift was next to those doors on the right side. He entered the lift and after the doors closed with him alone inside, he put his brass key into the hole at the bottom of the control panel. As soon as he turned the key, the lift began to descend to the third sub-basement. The indicator outside in the foyer gave no indication that the car had moved from the lobby level.

The brightly painted brick walls of the sub-basement gave the place a World War Two ambience. It was the correct message, for these quarters had been built in the late thirties on orders from the Lord of the Admiralty just in case that crazy Austrian might attract enough of a following to become a problem.

Cosby walked twenty yards down the hall to the right and opened a door with a simple "16" on it. Morford's desk was just a few feet inside the door and he looked up as Cosby entered. He got to his feet and came to Cosby swiftly.

"Sorry to have called you in on a Saturday afternoon, sir, but we wanted you to get a secure briefing on this so you could decide what to do."

"Don't fret, Morford. You did the right thing. What is up?"

"Sir, Admiral Staker sent word that a Boeing 777, with two hundred thirty nine on board, departed Kuala Lumpur four hours ago. Just after it was handed off by Lumpur radar control to Ho Chi Minh control, it ceased to transmit transponder returns. It is still emitting ACARS pings hourly, but no one can raise it by radio. Shortly after that, it ceased to

103

respond to ACARS in the normal manner, but continues to indicate that the engines are running."

"Very suspicious that it would have an upset during the hand off. Perfect chance to buy a little time before the new controller would become suspicious. Any information on the course it took after the upset?"

"ACARS will not get another ping for about another forty minutes. The first ping was so close to the position where the handoff occurred that it does not reveal much. The satellite is not pinpoint accurate since it is using Doppler to determine the range and azimuth."

"Do you have our analysts up to speed?"

"Yes, sir, they know as much as I have told you."

"What about the civil authorities. What have they said?"

"Malaysian authorities have just announced the plane did not report. There is a frenzy among the news people, worldwide."

"Any British nationals on board?"

"We don't know, but we suspect that there will be only a few, if any. Most of the passengers are thought to be Chinese returning to Beijing. The flight was to continue on to Frankfurt, so there are thought to be several Europeans on board."

"Well, it could be a catastrophic accidental depressurization, but the timing is very suspicious. I would think it looks more like pilot diversion or a hijacking."

"How much fuel was on board?" asked Cosby.

"We don't know, sir. The civil authorities either do not know or aren't releasing that information."

"I cannot believe that a competent airline would have a 777 on an international flight over water without knowing exactly how much fuel was on board. Keep on that and let me know as soon as you find out. What is the maximum range of the aircraft?"

"Sir, it is a 777-200 ER, for extended range. The Boeing site says that the fuel capacity is forty five thousand two hundred gallons. It has a range of seven thousand seven hundred nautical miles."

"Then, it could reach us, couldn't it?"

"Yes, sir, with no adverse winds it could."

"If you or your replacement acquire any information that it is headed this way, issue an alert to the Home Force."

"Yes, sir, will do."

"Cosby walked over to get a clear view of the huge chart on the screen. A technician had placed a radius around where the plane last reported. The television people were only using a radius the same distance as Beijing without reporting the plane's capability.

"Probably best," thought Cosby. "No need to alarm people just yet."

He settled into a large overstuffed leather chair to watch the information accumulate on the big screen and ancillary screens as the technicians hustled to post what they were acquiring.

Chapter 20

Chief Warrant Officer Fisher and his five crew members slipped over the side of the Reuben James and got into their inflatable. It was very dark due to a low overcast. Once securely aboard they started the outboard and motored away from the Reuben James into the dark. In twenty minutes, they spotted what they came for. Each of the men had his night vision goggles on. The Iranian fishing boat was motoring along at minimum speed, with its running lights on. It was clearly within Iranian territory and was just cruising slowly northward in the night. Sergeant Blair brought the inflatable into the path of the oncoming fishing boat and as the boat got up to the inflatable, the crew used hooked ladders and ropes to get on board as quietly as they could. Blair let the black inflatable drift into the wake of the fishing boat until it was about a hundred yards off. It must have been a very frightening experience to see armed men in black wet suits suddenly appear on their boat. The sailors were completely surprised.

Fisher and his men took the fishermen as prisoners and put plastic ties on their wrists and took them to the fore deck. They brought all four of them forward. Blair, who was watching closely saw them appear and brought the inflatable forward alongside the fishing boat. The fishing boat was about forty feet long and diesel powered. It was not fast at all, but was just what they needed.

The men got the Iranians into the inflatable and then put black bags over their heads and Blair and one other man motored off to take the captured sailors to the Reuben James.

Fisher took out his handheld transceiver and broadcast: "Jumbo, jumbo."

One of the men aimed an infrared strobe toward the southwest. In a few minutes, Lieutenant (JG) Bosley arrived in another inflatable with his crew of Aerial Observation technicians and quickly boarded the fishing boat. One of the men in Fisher's crew took the helm and continued motoring slowly north. He had a handheld GPS receiver to help him establish a course during the night.

As soon as the technicians were safely on board, Fisher and Blair got into the inflatable that brought the technicians and started back to the Reuben James.

Below decks, the technicians, Davis, Joyce and Lane, began assembling their gear and some of the drone aircraft they had brought. The drones were black in color, had a wingspan of about four feet and were powered by muffled engines commonly found on radio controlled model airplanes.

When they had tested the television cameras on the drones and found all in order, Bosley radioed the

Reuben James with the code words: "Marathon, marathon."

The Reuben James radioed Captain Warshovsky on the Reagan by scrambler. Captain Warshovsky told the Reuben James's captain, Commander Beane, to send all further communications to Lero on a discrete frequency. Lero was to oversee the coming surveillance effort and report, while Captain Warshovsky busied himself with other pressing matters.

They had set up a little booth in a corner of the CIC for Lero, He had a chair and a small desk to make notes on. He picked up the headset and keyed the mike.

"Reuben James," this is Lero. "Instruct Marathon to proceed as planned."

"Roger, Lero. Reuben James will advise Marathon to proceed, standing by."

By now, Fisher and his boat load of technicians and SEALS were within ten miles of the Pakistani coast. It was just past midnight, local time. Fisher told the helmsman to continue at a slow speed toward the harbor opening at Karachi.

When the boat got within three miles of the harbor mouth, Fisher gave the go-ahead to the technicians to launch the first drone. In a few minutes, they brought it to the deck, attached the wing and its control cables and got the motor started. The wind was sweeping toward the shore, so they took advantage of a nice tailwind to launch the first drone. Once it was gone, the helmsman turned to the west and continued a slow cruise. The technicians below decks watched the GPS read out on where the drone was and the camera feed from the drone, which now only displayed an occasional bright point of light and no visibility toward the ocean below. Once the drone got over land they could see buildings and roads below it even though there was nothing directly ahead. After the drone had progressed about ten miles inland, they began to see outlines of what they were looking for. The large Jinnah airport lay ahead with its long parallel runways. As things came into sharper view, they could see the Ispahani hangar. It stood out due to its immense size. It was large enough to accommodate the largest airliners.

"Make sure the camera is recording," ordered Fisher. We will watch the live feed and pass it along to Lero by satellite, but we need to record as well."

"Roger, sir, we are recording," said Davis.

"Can you tell from the GPS what the winds are at the height the drone is operating?" asked Fisher.

"Yes, sir, the wind is currently eleven knots from two eight zero degrees. If we approach the hangar on a heading of two eight zero degrees, we can virtually hover close by enough to get some footage through the windows. With all the noise at the airport, there will be excellent cover, too."

"See what you can do. If things get difficult, go around for another pass. This is good stuff."

Chapter 21

(The following is translated from Georgian, a dialect of Russian.)

At about 2:45 local time, a two and a half ton truck pulled up to the door of the old warehouse on Kvemo Street in Tiblisi. (Georgia) It was followed by a black Zlin sedan. The passenger in the back seat of the Zlin got out when the two vehicles stopped and went to the side of the large door. At about shoulder height, he inserted a large eight inch long key and rotated it clockwise a quarter turn. The lock unlatched and he withdrew the key. In ten seconds, the door automatically began to raise. When he had sufficient clearance, he went in on the right side and used his flashlight to light his way. About fifty yards back, he stopped in front of a large steel-fenced area of the warehouse. Using another, smaller key, he opened the lock on the gate and swung it fully open. There were three crates on the floor, elevated by four-by-four chocks at each end. Each crate was about two feet high, two feet wide and ten feet long.

Colonel Gori turned to the waiting sergeant and said, "Load all three in the truck."

Sergeant Shida motioned to his men to come forward. Using the dollies nearby, they gently lifted the first crate and rolled it on the dolly to the truck, which by now had turned around and backed into the warehouse. It took almost an hour for the crew to load the crates, but when they were finished, Sergeant Shida went out to the sedan and came to attention outside the closed rear window. Colonel Gori lowered the window and the Sergeant reported that the crates were all on board.

"Very well," said Colonel Gori and got out and went into the warehouse again to lock the gate. All the men came out as he went in and they got into the truck. Colonel Gori was the last one out of the warehouse and he lowered the front door using the control on the wall near the opening. When the door had lowered, he went over and assured that it was locked by inserting his key and rotating it one quarter turn counterclockwise. Then he walked quickly to his waiting car, his breath steaming in the sub-freezing night. In a couple of minutes, the car and the truck were gone.

In a half hour, the truck and car pulled up along side an Ata airlines IL-96M airplane at the Tiblisi airport. Colonel Gori watched from the heated comfort of his car as the men loaded the crates into the cargo hold of the airliner. When they were finished and Shida made his report of that, Colonel Gori said: "Good work, Yuri. Take the car and the truck back to the compound. Give the men an extra ration of vodka. See you in a week or so."

"Thank you, Colonel. See you soon," said Shida, and he turned on his heel and strode toward the truck and the waiting men.

Colonel Gori took a suitcase from the trunk of the car and, using the ladder nearby, boarded the airliner as it sat in the darkened hangar. When the flight crew reported for duty two hours later, they were surprised to see that they already had a first class passenger. When he showed them his ticket and his ID, they knew they were to ask no questions. Even though the ID was only a regular military ID, the time and manner of his boarding gave a clue that they were dealing with a KGB officer.

In a few minutes, the massive doors of the hangar began to open. A tug came in from the terminal and attached to the nose landing gear, and in a few minutes, towed the airliner out of the hangar and to a gate at the terminal.

After sitting there for a short while, the public address system rasped and a female voice said: "Good morning, Ladies and Gentlemen, Ari Airlines Flight 413 to Tehran, Iran, is now loading at gate seven. Please have your boarding passes ready as you check in."

In due time, the airliner made a regular departure from Tiblisi and climbed to its cruising altitude.

"Good evening, Ladies and Gentlemen, Announcing the arrival of Ari Airlines Flight four one three from Tiblisi, Georgia at gate thirty one."

After all the passengers had de-planed, including Colonel Gori, the flight crew and flight attendants left the aircraft and went into the terminal to catch their rides to their hotels. The terminal crew backed the airway away from the airliner and the tug pulled the airplane across the airport to the military hangar instead of the Ari Airlines hangar.

Colonel Gori was met by Captain Abasha of the Republican Guard and escorted to a military automobile for his trip across the airport to the military hangar. By the time they got there, the airliner had already been towed into the hangar and the great doors were closed. Gori and Abasha entered a smaller regular door in the side of the hangar. The driver took the car back to the terminal.

"The plan seems to be going well, so far, Colonel Gori. You and I will board this aircraft here in the hangar and will fly to Karachi on the regular morning flight which leaves in three hours and a half. I have our tickets, so we can just go in and get our seats and take a nap until the plane is towed to the passenger terminal. Our operatives have placed information in the boarding computer of the airline to show that you and I boarded regularly and are seated in first class."

"This is good," said Colonel Gori. "I could use a nap before the flight ."

They settled into their seats, Gori in A-3 and Abasha in D-5.

Chapter 22

"General Staker, for you, Mr. President," said the aide, handing him the headset:

"History is strewn with debris of battles that the planners never thought would happen. Guessing what the other side will do has always been a very inexact science. What we know now is that Flight 370 was hijacked and flown to Karachi. The aircraft is in the Ispahani Hangar and has been there for approximately six hours. We do not know who has control of the aircraft or how many people are working on the airplane in the hangar. Our Aerial Surveillance Squad is on a commandeered Pakistani fishing boat with SEALS for security, and they are in position off the shore of Karachi. They have dispatched a small drone to fly past the hangar and try to get a look in the windows. Images of the first pass show nothing of intelligence value to us."

"What do your analysts think at this point?"

"Our people believe that the list of controlling organizations probably includes a branch of Al Qaeda, Chechen separatists, Hezbollah and its Iranian controllers, Taliban, and Pakistani nationalists. They believe that if the aircraft is under the control of Al Qaeda, their intention is to hit the United States, either a major population center like New York, or Washington, the seat of government. They believe if the aircraft is under the control of

Chechen separatists, they intend to hit Moscow. That is a very scary prospect, because if they succeed or even if they get close to unleashing some deadly kind of weapon, nuclear, chemical or biological or all of the above, the Russians will assume, erroneously, that it is a strike by the United States and Russia will unleash all of its ICBMs from land bases and submarines. Since our detection systems will doubtless detect the launches promptly, our government will have to decide very quickly if it wants to attack with our offensive missiles while our defensive missiles attempt to take out what we can of their inbound missiles. This, as I said, is very scary."

If the controllers are Hezbollah and Iran, they probably will try to wipe out Israel as they have threatened for decades. If they use a nuke, it will probably kill almost all of the Palestinians, too.

Our people think there is a slight chance that the controllers are Pakistani separatists who will launch the aircraft against India. With a nuke or two or more and chemical and biological weapons, they could do serious damage to India.

Lero and the President were listening to that analysis in far apart circumstances. Lero was on the Reagan, about one hundred fifty miles south of Karachi and the President was in the Situation Room in the basement of the White House.

"Thank you, General Staker, please keep me advised as you acquire information. I will be standing by either here or in the Oval Office."

"Yes, Mr. President. Thank you," said Staker, and hung up the headset.

Chapter 23

While Colonel Gori and Colonel Abashi were waiting for the plane to be towed from the hangar to the regular boarding gate at Khomeini Airport, they had a chance to talk.

"As soon as we make the transfer at Karachi, we will excuse you so you can slip back into Russia without detection. The deposit to your account in the Cayman Islands will be made as soon as our people accept the shipment in the Aspahani Hangar. So far, it appears that none of our activities have been observed or detected," said Colonel Abashi.

"Good," said Colonel Gori. "As you might imagine, I have many people to compensate for their participation in this venture. I would request that your people remove all external marking from the devices and incinerate the wood crate material as soon as practical. My own belief is that your people will use these devices to hit either Israel or the United States. If you care to share any information, I will keep it personal, but I am just curious."

"Regrettably, they have not shared that information with me. I agree, it is most probable, given the make-up of the planning committee, that they will use these devices and chemical and biological weapons to hit the United States. The long range of the aircraft would be wasted on a strike on Israel, don't you think?" asked Colonel Abashi.

"Yes, the range of the aircraft makes it feasible to hit any site in the United States east of the Mississippi River. What a prospect!" said Colonel Gori.

"In any case, you and your people are to be congratulated on a smooth and expeditious project. Nicely done, Valentin," said Colonel Abashi.

"Thank you for your kind assessment. I wish your people success. I and my people will disappear on regularly scheduled flights shortly after the hand off."

They settled into their first class seats to catch a quick nap before the crew arrived. The huge hangar was absolutely silent.

Chapter 24

"Captain Schultz, as G-2 for this task force, I need to make you aware of my mission and ask your help. President Thompson has placed me in charge of the response to a situation that has developed over the last seventy two hours. Code Name for our Mission is Cherokee. We think that that Malaysian Airliner that disappeared was actually hijacked by either the pilots or hijackers who were qualified pilots and flown to a hangar on the Karachi Airport. Our suspicions at this time are that the people in control of the aircraft are going to dispose of the bodies of the passengers and their luggage, then repaint the aircraft in the livery of a regular airliner and use it to make a terror strike. At this time we don't know who is in charge, so we must plan for any of the contingencies that our analyst believe are the most probable. I need you to coordinate the preparation of aircraft to possibly shoot down this aircraft once we determine which direction it takes out of Karachi. The target could, of course, be anything, but we think the most probable targets are New York, Washington, London, Delhi, Tel Aviv and Moscow. We are going to need to have long range interceptors at the ready over a wide swath of geography. Knowing that your target is a Boeing 777-200ER, what do you think we should do?" asked Lero.

"Well, if they seem to be going toward Tel Aviv, we will have to react quickly. The distance toTel Aviv from Karachi is only eight hundred miles. The only safe place to shoot the plane down is over water, so that whatever weapons they have on board will be buried at sea and not damage or contaminate the area of the crash. We have our own task force here on the Reagan with seventy five F-15s. We need to alert the G-2 on the Enterprise which is in the eastern Mediterranean so they can provide cover, too. In case we discern that they are targeting London, we would need to shoot the plane down over the English Channel. If, indeed, they are targeting the United States, we would shoot it down over the central Atlantic, far out of radar contact and over deep water. If they go for Moscow, we will have to alert the Russian authorities and let them defend themselves. Of course, they are so paranoid that they may suspect that we are manipulating this strike under the cover of some fanatic group like the Chechen separatists. If the plane slips through and completes its attack on Moscow, they may retaliate against us, thinking that we were responsible. This is really scary. How many people know about this situation?" Schultz asked.

"The President, his National Security Advisor, the CIA and the NSA and their auxiliaries, Admiral Staker, you and I and members of my team, which is quite small," said Lero.

"No need to fill the airways with a lot of chatter about this, even with scramblers, someone might detect the increased activity and become suspicious that we are onto them," said Schultz.

"How would you propose to contact the Russians, if we have to?" asked Schultz.

"I will rely on Jefe, my mentor and the previous head of our group. He has extensive contacts in Russia as well as many other places. They talk regularly, mostly just small talk, but they keep the line of communication open in case something like this comes up," said Lero.

"That is good to know," said Schultz. "By the way, call me Bud if you want."

"Thanks, Bud," said Lero.

"Where is Jefe now," asked Schultz.

"Jefe is at Ovda Air Base in Israel," said Lero. "Close enough to meet face to face with his Russian counterpart somewhere if need be."

"There are so many possibilities here," said Schultz. We need to have a wide set of nets ready. Is it OK if I alert my counterparts on the Enterprise and Atlantic Fleet?" asked Schultz.

"Yes, but tell them that this must be kept close to the vest," added Lero.

"Thank you for involving me in this. I will give you my best effort," said Schultz.

With that, they left the secure room and each went his separate ways to get on with preparations.

Chapter 25

"Major Gilan?"asked Captain Shareza.

"Yes, what is it?" asked Gilan.

The trucks with the cylinders have arrived. I did not want to open the doors again without your permission. We must be very careful about being observed."

"You are correct, Captain. We took a risk opening the doors earlier for the trucks to take the bodies and luggage out. Another opening might raise suspicions, but we cannot turn off the lights in the hangar. It would startle the workers and it would take ten minutes for the mercury vapor lights to strike arcs and begin to light us up again. Tell Captain Hossein to hold the trucks where he is. I will go out and make an inspection of the situation. Go with me, so you may radio Hossein if all is well."

Shahreza saluted and followed Gilan.

They went out a side door from an office room and turned out the lights before they opened the door in the side of the hangar building. In the heavy seashore humidity, there was already a layer of fog near the ground and visibility was about a quarter of a mile. Even though the airport was busy, it was "normal" busy and Gilan instructed Shareza to radio Hossein that it was OK to bring the three trucks into the hangar. They ordered the crew to open the door just enough to clear the trucks and to shut the doors as soon as the trucks were inside.

With all the ambient noise of distant airplanes taking off and taxiing to the terminal, Major Gilan did not notice the black drone that flew past them about a hundred feet above the tarmac. It only made one pass and returned south out of the airport area.

The images from the drone were live broadcast back to the fishing boat where the Aerial Observation team immediately fed the broadcast as they recorded it to Lero on the Reagan and to Admiral Staker at CIA and General Behm at NSA. Analysts went to work right away with still pictures taken from the footage to analyze what was in the hangar and what was being done in the hangar. Staker ordered the Aerial Observation squad to retrieve the drone for fear of alerting those it was observing.

About three AM, local time, Ari airlines flight 342 arrived from Tehran. After it discharged its passengers and crew, a tug towed it to a darkened spot adjacent to the hangar. Staker and Lero had thought it was worth the risk to try another drone flight since they had waited two hours since the last flight. When the drone flew by the Ari airliner, they could see that suspicious crates were being removed by fork lift trucks from the cargo hold of the Airliner. Analysts quickly identified the crates as similar to known design containers of Russian medium yield nuclear weapons. There were three crates.

Staker alerted Central Command headquarters and General Hammond, the commander was brought up to speed quickly. He then had his communications officer get him a telephone patch to Lero and to General Behm at NSA.

Once the line was established, he said: "This is Red Cloud, our people have determined that the crates are most likely medium yield Russian nuclear weapons, probably Type C7. Now we really know that those who have that aircraft are up to no good. Lero, plan for an aerial interdiction of that aircraft. If it heads for Israel, we will notify the Israelis and shoot it down over the desert somewhere. If it heads for the U.S. we will have a fighter from the Enterprise intercept it and shoot it down over the Atlantic. If it heads for Russia, we will notify the Russians and shoot it down before it gets to Russia. We cannot wait long enough to allow the Russians to come to the false conclusion that we are behind this. If we only knew which group was behind the attack, we could focus more. Since we do not, plan for any contingency you think has even a small probability. Do you both have the assets you need to carry out any of these contingencies?"

"Admiral Staker spoke first. "We think we have the assets we will need, sir. We have three aircraft carriers: one here in the Indian Ocean about a hundred miles off shore from Karachi, the Enterprise in the Med, and the Bush in the Atlantic about three hundred miles southwest of Liverpool. We have Aegis class destroyers in all of those positions, too, and there are three nuclear subs arrayed so that they are near enough to the carriers to be of help if necessary. The whole team is on alert, sir."

"I think we only have a few hours to figure out how to react. Keep me advised of any development, gentlemen."

"Yes, sir," said Lero and Admiral Staker almost together. The line disconnected.

Chapter 26

Lero had the coms sailor dial a special number on the satellite network. It rang four times before a male voice answered.

"Yes?" he said.

The coms sailor nodded to Lero. Lero keyed his headset and said, "Lero to speak to General Haim, please."

"One moment," the male voice said.

In a few seconds, General Haim came on: "This is General Haim, say the word."

Lero said: "Houston."

"Good evening, my friend, to what do I owe the honor of this call?"

"General Haim, I have some news. We have tracked the missing airliner to a hangar on the Karachi Airport. We believe that a terrorist group is outfitting the aircraft with weapons of mass destruction and intends to use the aircraft for a terror strike."

"Thank you, Lero. We were aware that the aircraft was missing, but knew very little else."

"The President has put me in charge of coordinating our response. I am on the carrier Reagan in the Indian Ocean about a hundred miles south of Karachi. We have other assets alerted to deal with this situation, too. Our analysts believe there is a small probability that they will try to hit Israel with this weapon. We have succeeded in getting some footage from a drone that flew across the airport and got a peek inside the hangar. I would propose to feed our current information to you if you will have your intel people contact Central Command coms and they can set up the link. All of our people believe that this is a very dangerous situation."

"Thank you, Lero. I appreciate your calling me so promptly. We would very much appreciate being in on the intel feed. I will have my intel coms people get in touch with Central Command coms immediately. If you need us to take any action, please call me immediately. I will stand by on this number until further notice. I agree with your analysts that the intended target will be indicated by the identity of the group that has control of the plane. Call me whenever you need to. Thanks, very much."

Lero said: "I will be standing by at this number also. I will advise of any developments. Thank you, sir. Good evening."

Chapter 27

(On board the U.S. Aircraft carrier George Herbert Walker Bush, in the Atlantic about three hundred nautical miles southwest of Liverpool.)

"Commander Marion, this is Captain Hollyfield. We have a developing situation. I want two F/A 18s on the catapults until further notice. Have the pilots remain in the aircraft on two hour shifts. Change out one aircraft at a time. The aircraft are to be fully fueled, of course, and fully armed with guns and missiles. I will brief you and your pilots as soon as I can get to your ready room."

"Roger, sir. I will have my first two pilots here when you get here."

Chapter 28

According to plan, the freighter lay off shore of
Karachi until it could arrive after dark. As it eased
into its position at the dock, a large box truck with
Federal Express markings moved up next to the
door in the side of the ship. After the door opened,
the truck backed up so its open end was at the
doorway. Inside, a crew member started a lift truck
and moved over adjacent to the three crates near
the forward bulkhead. An efficient crew had marked
the center of gravity on the outside when they
removed the Russian markings by painting over
them. Now the crates had stenciled lettering that
indicated that they were Italian manufactured
machine parts. The LPG fueled lift truck worked
very quietly and hefted the first crate. It backed
away from the forward bulkhead and lowered the
crate so that it was only a few inches from the floor.
Then the driver turned and took the crate over to the
open door. The driver carefully placed one end of
the crate on the rollers that had been placed on the
floor of the truck. Helpers then placed jacks under
the other end of the crate, so the lift truck could
back away. The lift truck driver then maneuvered
around to the end of the crate and, after closing up
the distance between the forks, gently lifted the
outside end of the crate. Once he had the crate up
on his forks, he eased it forward on the rollers until it
was completely in the truck. Then he and his
helpers did the same for the second and third

crates. Once they were loaded, three men got in the cab of the truck and it left the dock. It slowly meandered through the tight streets of Karachi northeastward toward the Jinnah Airport. The trip took more than an hour and they were grateful that, because it was late at night, there was little traffic. At the freight terminal gate, the driver pulled up to the gatehouse.

"Hello, Mahmud. Working late tonight?" asked the gate keeper, Saeed.

"Yeah," said Mahmud,. "We drive whenever they want us to."

"Where are you taking this load, so I can log it in?" asked Saeed.

"Ari Airlines hangar. This load is going to Tehran."

"OK," said Saeed and waved Mahmud through.

The truck went directly to the Ari Airlines hangar, paused long enough for the crew to have unloaded the truck, which they did not, and then slowly made its way to the Isfahani hangar. When Mahmud pulled up to the small door for pedestrians, the sentry saw him and signaled to the men at the main doors to open them just enough to let the truck in. As soon as the truck entered, the doors closed.

By the time they pulled the truck up to the cargo door of the 777, Colonel Rawal was there. He thanked Mahmud and his two helpers and asked them to help his crew load the crates in the cargo hold. The crew brought around their lift truck and the men reversed the process of loading, this time putting the crates in the airplane's cargo hold.

They worked promptly and when they were finished, Colonel Rawal told them to take the truck back to its terminal. Mahmud drove the truck out of the large hangar door and headed for the gate.

Rawal told the technician to set the Latitude and longitude on each of the devices at 38.8878North and 77.009West. Once the LED readout indicated those figures, he told the technician to close up the cover. Once that was done, they pulled the dark canvas tarpaulin over the devices and he and the technician went back out the cargo bay door and down the ladder to the floor of the hangar.

Chapter 29

Lero thought the situation required quick action. He called Jefe on the satellite phone.

Jefe answered on the fourth ring. He was gazing over the lip of the porch wall at his favorite hide out in Sharm El Sheik.

Now, the two had changed chairs, so to speak. When Jefe answered, Lero said, "Say the word."

Jefe dutifully replied "Chesapeake." Now they both knew to whom they were talking.

"Do we have any assets in Karachi? Preferably a taxi-cab driver?

"Yes, it happens that we have a man in Karachi who drives a taxi. What do you need?

We know that they have the item in the coop at Whiskey 7. I need to penetrate the coop. I plan to take Jean with me to look like tourists. The situation is coming to a boil and I fear they will fly soon. We have high cover on stand-by for the contingencies that we can foresee, but it clearly would be better if we could get on board."

"I understand. What is your schedule so I can alert our man?

I plan to have the Poseidon stop for fuel at Ahmedabad. She will deplane. I will meet her there and we will catch the 3:40 flight on Air India to Karachi. If you could take care of tickets and reservations, I would appreciate it. Mr. Dan and Mrs. Sue Roman."

"Anything else you need?" asked Jefe.

"No, if you cannot do the tickets, advise this number. Thank you, sir."

"Will do. Good luck. Tell me what you can when you can."

They both hung up.

Lero turned to the radio console in the CIC of the Reagan. "Navy 41516, this is Gipper. Can you land for fuel at Ahmedabad before two o'clock local time?"

"Roger, Gipper, 516 will stop for fuel at Ahmedabad shortly before 2.

"Thank you, five one six. Plan on de-planing your passenger there, too. Gipper out."

Now, to get some gear ready. Lero called the Quartermaster on the intercom.

"Lieutenant Perski, this is Lero. Can you come to CIC?"

"Yes, sir. Be there in ten minutes."

"OK. Thanks."

"Perk, we need some special clothes for a mission. I need a civilian suit, size forty two. Trousers thirty six by thirty. Shirt size sixteen. Sleeves thirty four/thirty five. Shoes size ten D, if you can. I need a woman's dark skirt, waist size 24 and a gray blouse size 8 and some dark flat heel shoes. I need a suitcase. On the large side. Color dark if you can. I need two pairs of dark coveralls. Black or navy blue. One for me and one for a lady who is five four and one hundred ten pounds. I need running shoes for her, too. Size six C, if you can. I need a baton. I also need a pharmaceutical pack with six styrettes of anesthetic and six with a terminal dose. I want the paint ball pistol with a dozen anesthetic darts, and I will need some Dramamine, just in case. I need six of those spray cans of immobilizing spray. I want a brain bag with all the current aeronautical charts for South Asia, Europe and the Atlantic Area. We will have to go through the boarding inspection at Ahmedabad Airport, so see if you can get us diplomatic visas, please. All that gear would get us stopped at boarding inspection."

"Will do, sir," said Perk, as he finished making notes. "How soon do you need this equipment?"

I need to depart on a COD within the hour. Can you do that?"

"I will report to you as soon as I have the gear and I will tell you if I cannot do it in time."

"Good enough," said Lero. "Thanks."

Perski turned on his heel and hustled down the companionway.

Lero dialed Jefe again.

"Say the word," he said as Jefe answered.

Jefe said the word and then Lero said, "I forgot to ask if our asset there could provide us a couple of handguns and a Heckler and Koch nine millimeter automatic weapon with five loaded magazines."

"I will ask him to do so and will advise if he is unable. If you do not hear from me by the time you get to Ahmedabad, assume that he has the weapons in his taxicab."

"Thanks, see you soon, I hope."

"Be careful, see you soon."

They hung up.

"Chief, can you get me a ride on a COD, destination Ahmedabad, within the hour?"

"Can do, sir. Fifty minutes. Will you be alone?"

"Yes, thank you, Chief."

Chief Hunley pushed his intercom button for the pilot's ready room.

"I need crew for a COD, destination Ahmedabad, leaving in forty minutes."

There was a pause of about ten seconds.

"Chief. We will have Olsen and Carolla ready to go by then. Anything else?"

"No, that will be fine. Thanks."

"Flight Ops, Commander Blake," said the deep voice.

"Commander Blake, this is Lieutenant Perski. Can you have a COD ready to go in forty minutes, destination Ahmedabad?"

"Can do, Perk. Who are the passengers?"

"Just Lero. Quick round trip. Book this flight to Lero's account."

"Will do, Perk. See you later."

They both hung up.

Lero went to his temporary quarters near the CIC. Lieutenant Perski and a seaman appeared at his door in about twenty minutes. They had the gear that he had ordered, so he changed then into the civilian clothes and checked everything.

"Thanks, Perk. It is just fine."

Perk said, "I know that you are involved in something we cannot discuss. I perceive that what you are about to do is dangerous. Best wishes, sir. I will be praying for you."

"Thanks, Perk. You have been a great help. I will let you know when we are in the clear. Thanks for the prayers."

They shook hands, eye to eye.

The seaman stayed and helped Lero up the companionway with his luggage. They stepped out onto the flight deck. There was a fine rain falling across the deck with a light wind. They walked to the Carrier On Board Delivery aircraft. Since he was the only passenger, as soon as he climbed aboard, they shut the door against the rain.

The pilot said over the intercom, "Welcome aboard Arabian Sea Night Hawk airlines. We will be flying over La Brea, Asuza and Cucamonga tonight, but we will be landing at Ahmedabad. Welcome aboard."

Lero laughed at the reference to Cucamonga and Asuza. He recalled, at a time long before the pilot was born, that the Jack Benny program contained those words, but they referred to train stops north of Hollywood.

Lero could not hear it, but Lieutenant Olson was on the radio to the Air Boss getting his clearance and departure briefing. As Lero watched the rain drops streak across his window, the pilots started the starboard engine. He pulled his seat belt tight and waited.

The COD taxied into position. Lero could feel and hear the line crew attach the catapult hook to the nose gear.

In a couple of minutes, the pilot said on the intercom.

"Prepare for catapult. Seat belt tight. Here we go."

About forty seconds later, the aircraft surged ahead on the steam catapult. In one hundred forty feet it accelerated to about one hundred knots. I was hurled into the night and immediately began its climb.

Chapter 30

The flight through a dark and cloudy night was about an hour and ten minutes. Clearance had been arranged by diplomatic exchange for the aircraft and the flight to Ahmedabad, so it went smoothly.

"Ahmedabad approach, United States Navy 447135 is approximately eighty nautical south west of Ammedabad, level at eleven thousand feet, squawking twelve hundred, landing Ahmedabad, requesting landing clearance."

"U.S. Navy 447135, this is Ahmedabad approach radar, squawk 3355 and ident. Maintain eleven thousand. Fly heading zero six five."

"Roger, Ahmedabad approach, 447135 is squawking 3355, maintaining eleven thousand and turning right to zero six five degrees."

"447135, you are in radar contact."

"Roger, 135."

In another twenty five minutes, the COD was cleared to land on Runway Seven and shortly thereafter, did so.

When Lero stepped onto the tarmac, he could see the Posiedon P-7 at an opposite tie down position. He asked the pilots to keep his luggage until he returned to the plane and he walked over the hundred yards to the P-7. As he got within about thirty yards, a Naval officer appeared at the head of the stairs and motioned him aboard. As he stepped into the P-7, Jean appeared from the rear compartment. They hugged warmly.

Lero asked the officer if there were a place where he and Jean could sit and plan their next move, and the officer showed them to a compartment near the front which was full of radio equipment, but had a small table surrounded by closely bunched chairs. It was ideal for their purpose and Lero and Jean slipped into opposing seats.

"I am so glad to see you," he said and reached for her hand. "How are you doing?"

"I'm fine, really," she said. "They have been very hospitable. I have been able to help them monitor air and sea traffic. Why did you want me to meet you here?"

Lero briefed her on everything they knew about the plane and the hangar, the theories about who was in charge and what they intended to do with the plane and he told her in general terms what military assets were in place and the fact that the President had put him in charge of efforts to bring this crisis to a good end. He told her what he wanted her to do and then he said, "Jean, you are so dear to me. I would not put you in danger if it were my decision, but the President believes that your presence with me will give credibility to our mission since we must deceive some pretty canny characters. There is no getting around the fact that this is dangerous work and you may have to use lethal force. If you have any qualms about going, say so and I will get a Navy nurse or some other woman officer to go with me. Your name for this part of the mission is Sue Roman. My name will be Dan Roman. We have tickets on Air India flight 453 to Karachi which leaves in about an hour. I have arranged for our bags to be checked as diplomatic luggage so it will not be searched."

He then told her what all was in the luggage. Her eyes widened as he did so. Then he told her in detail what he planned to do. Afterward, he took both of her hands in his and said as tenderly as he could: "Please tell me how you feel about all this. I need your help, but I won't ask you to do this if you feel you cannot give this your best effort."

"When you came into my life, I knew that you were going to be a person into whom I could pour everything I had. I trusted you from the moment we shook hands that first time. If we have to die for our country, I would want it to be together," she said.

They stood up and hugged. They kissed tenderly.

He retrieved their "luggage" which was two medium sized roller equipped cases. They each took one and rolled them into the Fixed Base Operator's Lounge. Jean gave his hand a quick squeeze and she headed for the rest room. When she came back, he took his turn. When he came back out, she had an odd look on her face. He gave her a quizzical look and she said, "The ladies room is very nice. Do you suppose we could use it for a while? I am burning for you."

He followed her to the ladies room. Once inside, she edged up onto the counter next to the sink, wrapped her legs around him and very efficiently showed him how much she had missed him. When they left the ladies room later, he noticed a thin line of moisture fogging the lower margin of the mirror. As he watched her replace and adjust her clothing, he marveled at how beautiful she was. As they approached the door, he kissed her again.

Chapter 31

The Air India ticket agent was a tall very dark eyed woman who looked up as they approached.

"Mr. and Mrs. Dan Roman, tickets to Karachi, please."

"Yes, Mr. Roman, your reservations are confirmed and your luggage has been checked through. Here are your boarding passes. The aircraft will arrive presently, and after the passengers de-plane, they will call for your boarding. Have a pleasant flight."

Lero nodded and said, simply: "Thank you," and took the boarding passes.

He and Jean sat in the boarding section of seats next to their gate. He watched the Airbus 320 taxi up and stop with its nose about twenty feet from the glass.

"Your attention please, Air India Flight 340 to Karachi has arrived. Boarding will commence in twenty minutes."

As they got in line to board, they followed a distinguished looking Sikh gentleman and his lady companion, who, in the Indian custom, walked behind him. About eighty people got off of the flight and, in a few minutes, they called for boarding of the first class passengers. Lero and Jean had agreed that they would not discuss anything about the mission on the plane unless it was behind a cupped hand next to the ear of the hearer. Security had to be very tight.

The flight to Karachi left close to on time and the flight was uneventful and smooth. The twin engine Airbus ate up the distance to Karachi in an hour and twenty minutes. The flight attendants served dinner in flight and they enjoyed a nice lightly seasoned lamb curry and rice dinner.

The plane was filled with an international mixture of passengers. They blended in, looking like average tourists. When they de-planed, the flight attendant said that their luggage would be available in about twenty minutes. Even though most of the passengers were continuing on to Dubai, all passengers were de-planed so the ground crew could refresh the interior with a rapid vacuuming and refilling of the drink refrigerator and water bottles and remove the table ware from the in-flight meal. It all took place in a well choreographed manner as Lero and Jean made their way from their seats to the luggage return area.

Shortly after their luggage was deposited in the return area, a taxi driver approached them and asked if they wanted him to get their bags for them. Lero pointed out their bags and gave him the baggage checks so he could retrieve them. The luggage clerk nodded when the taxi driver showed him the stubs for the correct bags and he gathered them up and came back to where Lero and Jean were standing.

"My cab is the second one in line, number 562," he said.

It was a late model Mercedes, a light tan color. The driver put the bags in the trunk and opened the rear door for them to enter. Because he dared not to have left the engine running because of the theft potential, he restarted the engine and put the air conditioner onto recirculate to cool the car as quickly as possible. Since they were not being hurried by other traffic, as soon as he had started the engine, he turned to them and said: "My name is Rangit Jorhat. Jefe sent me to help you. I have the chart bag you requested in the trunk. What is the plan?"

Lero told Rangit and Jean how he planned to get a look at what was inside the hangar and get inside if possible. He asked Rangit to open the trunk for him so he could retrieve a small bag from one of the larger suitcases. He and Rangit returned to their seats and Lero showed both of them the weapons that were in the bag and how to use them. Then he gave the bag to Jean to hold during their first approach.

"How far is the hangar from here?" asked Lero.

"It is only about a mile, but with the traffic and complicated roadways, it will probably take us five minutes," said Rangit. "It is good that it is after dark for the first approach. Are you both ready?"

Lero glanced at Jean. She nodded to him.

Lero said, "We are ready, Rangit. We appreciate your help. Do you have a weapon or do you need one from us?"

"I have a nine millimeter handgun in the glove box," said Rangit. "I have a suppressor for it, too. Should I put the suppressor on now?"

"Yes, that would be a good idea. The less noise we make, the better."

Lero had a map of the hangar area. He leaned forward and showed it to Rangit.

"Can you bring us to this door on the west side of the hangar? We have determined that it affords the best opportunity."

"Certainly, there are vehicle access ways on all four sides of the hangar.

"If there is more than one guard at the door I want to use, this could get complicated. We may just need to talk a bit and withdraw to reconnoiter if there are several guards."

By now, they had moved almost a half mile. Traffic was still bumper to bumper and slow, with lots of horn blowing by the impatient taxi drivers. But, when they turned off of the regular exit road and onto an access road toward the hangar, they were suddenly the only vehicle within sight ahead.

Chapter 32

As they pulled up to the hangar, Rangit slowed so they could observe as much as possible. The windows they could see had been painted over with a light coat of white paint. It would pass the light from within, but not reveal any details.

"Clever work," thought Lero.

The hangar was over four hundred feet long and there were numerous pallets with spare jet engines and parts on them stacked along the west side of the hangar. The arrangement of the pallets prevented the guard at the south west corner from observing the guard at the middle door on that side.

Lero asked Rangit to pull them up to the middle door. Because the people in charge knew that too much armed presence outside the hangar would bring a curious airport policeman to check things out, the plotters had only a single guard at each door.

Rangit pulled up short of the door, so the guard could easily see that they seemed to present no threat. Lero got out and strode over to the guard.

Lero said in Urdu: "Good evening. I am Dan Roman. I am here to pick up Prince Ganda's aircraft and return it to him. It has been here for a "C" check inspection and maintenance."

While Lero was telling the guard this, Rangit got out and opened the taxi's trunk and began slowly taking out the bags. He opened the door and let Jean out. She got out and stretched and tried to look mildly curious but bored at the same time.

The guard said, "Mr. Roman, no one told me to expect you. Please wait here while I check with the manager to determine the location of your aircraft. What is the registration number of the aircraft?"

"The number is Victor Hotel Foxtrot Uniform November.

"Victor Hotel Foxtrot Uniform November," repeated the guard and he wrote the letters on his clip board. By now, Jean had walked over to Lero and put her arm through his arm and snuggled up to him. In the dark, the guard did not notice that she raised her right arm and pointed it at him. The anesthetic dart hit him in the left side of his neck about an inch down from his ear. He made no sound, but his eyes widened as he realized what had happened. He reached for his hand held radio to sound the alarm, but before he could do that, his eyes lowered and he crumpled. Lero caught him in mid-fall and held him up. Rangit quickly came over and they hustled the guard to the taxi. Rangit took off the guard's tunic and put it on and gathered up his hat from where it had fallen. Lero searched his pockets and retrieved his keys. He also took the Makarov pistol from his holster and refastened the flap. He handed the pistol to Rangit, who put it in his pocket quickly. Then they closed the trunk lid.   Both looked both ways to see if anyone had noticed their activities. No one was in sight.

Lero said to Rangit: "We will use his keys to enter here. We will try to check things out and return out this door within thirty minutes. If we are not out in thirty minutes. Leave this area and go back to the taxi line at the terminal. If you are there for more than thirty minutes, call Jefe and give him an update. Tell him we will contact him directly when we have a plan. We have a hand held transceiver and will use it only if necessary. Good luck."

Rangit replied: "I will dump the guard where he will not be discovered. How long will he be unconscious?"

"About an hour, give or take," said Lero.

"I will turn him over to our people, then let them keep him."

"Good plan. Thank you, Rangit. We could not have done this without you."

"I am glad to have helped. These are really bad people, Lero. Be extra careful. See you later, I hope."

They found the correct key on the keychain that they had taken from the guard. They they shook hands and Rangit went back to get in his taxicab.

Chapter 33

Before they opened the door, Lero briefed Jean on
his plan. She nodded and got hold of her rolling
suitcase. They slowly opened the door and found
that they would be entering an interior hallway that
led along the side of the hangar. It had small rooms
off of the side toward the hangar interior which were
used as offices and storage rooms. The hall was
dimly lit. They entered, turned left and went toward
the far end of the hall. The last door on the right was
unlocked. They ducked into it and in the dark,
realized that it was some sort of an office. There
was a window between it and the interior of the
hangar. Through the venetian blinds, they could
see what was going on inside.

Lero said to Jean: "They have painted over the old
paint, but I am convinced that is the missing
airplane. With all those people in there, it will be
impossible to take it or to disable it without being
observed. I think we should get on board and hide
and take action only after they take off. Do you
have your pharmaceutical pack?"

Jean nodded.

Look in that cabinet over there and see if there are
any coveralls.

She moved quickly to the cabinet. How he loved the way she moved.

There were several pairs of coveralls in the locker. Using her small penlight, she found two, one large and one medium and brought them to Lero.

"Good," he said. "See that scaffold toward the nose of the plane? If we could get up on it without being stopped, we might sneak into the cargo hold. The best hiding place would be the food lockers or the avionics bay in the nose. Check your dart pistol and make sure it is good to go."

While he continued to look for a place to enter and while he thought of a method to get them over to the scaffold, she checked the pistol again and put another dart in it.

"We are not going to be able to wheel our suitcases with us. I will try to get us a couple of tool boxes to put our equipment in so we will look like technicians when we try to get on board. Wait here."

Lero put on the larger coverall and a ball cap that was on the desk. He slipped out the door and went to the end of the hall. The door on the right at the end of the hall led to the main hangar. Along the wall were lockers for the technicians to change into coveralls and leave their gear. About fifty feet down the wall, he spotted a suitable tool box. He casually strode up to it and picked it up and returned to the hallway. He went back into the room with Jean, but he tapped their signal on the door, so she would know it was him and let him in.

In the next minutes, they went through their gear and transferred the essential equipment from their rolling suitcases to the tool kit. Lero took a moment to take the appropriate charts for central Asia from the "brain bag" and put them in the tool kit. The other equipment they took included their pistols, the H & K assault rifles with their folding stock and five extra magazines, six thermite charges, the rest of the anesthetic darts, two skeins of nylon rope, a dozen tie wraps, two rolls of duct tape, the transceiver, a dozen energy bars and eight quarts of G-2 Gatorade, his multi-tool and two locking blade knives. Last to go in were four pounds of plastic explosive and the timer with detonators. If they needed anything else, they would have to find it on board.

Lero looked at his watch. It was 2:38 AM, local time. Even in the middle of the night, workers poured over the aircraft, finishing up the repainting and loading canisters into the cargo hold.

He told Jean: "This will be risky. I love you so much. If you are pursued and get separated from me, consider using the pill. Don't let yourself be captured. Sorry to put you in danger, but this is critical. These people are bent on doing something huge and bad. A lot of people have been killed already and there may be thousands more if these people succeed. If I die tonight, my last thoughts will be of you."

She bit her lip and nodded. She kissed him softly and tenderly.

They put their suitcases into the locker and closed it. Then, they eased into the hallway. Lero was carrying the tool kit and she followed closely. He spotted another ball cap as they entered and gave it to her. With it on, she could pass for a guy. They walked at a normal pace directly to the scaffold that led to the forward cargo door. They made it all the way up and into the door before they encountered anyone. There was a mechanic, his coveralls spattered with the fresh paint just inside the door. Lero spoke to him in Urdu and said that they were to make sure that the commissary was fully stocked and get food for it if necessary. The mechanic told them to go ahead and watched as they went forward. In the dim light, the mechanic did not realize that Jean was not a guy. They used the forward hatch in the cargo bay bulkhead (wall) to enter the food storage and preparation area below the forward area of the aircraft. Beyond this compartment was the avionics bay with all the radio equipment of the aircraft. Through the small window in the hatch, Jean could see a guard enter the cargo bay. The mechanic spoke with him for a bit and then pointed to the compartment where Jean and Lero were. The mechanic went outside onto the scaffold as the guard approached the door. When he opened the door, Lero let him step inside before he hit him with the dart gun. As he crumpled to the floor, Lero dragged him to a locker along the wall. He took out the duct tape and tied his hands and feet and put tape over his mouth. Then the two of them hefted him into a food locker and shut the door. Lero collected the guard's pistol and hid it were they could retrieve it later if they needed to.

Chapter 34

Outside, Rangit looked at his watch and realized that more than thirty minutes had passed. He strode over to his taxicab and got in. He put the guard's hat on the passenger seat and laid his pistol under it. The guard in the trunk made no sound.

Rangit started the taxicab and motored slowly away. He passed completely around the hangar and went back out to the main access road to the terminal. On the way, he spotted a dumpster and stopped just beyond it. In the middle of the night, as dark as it was, no one saw him tape the guard's hands and feet and put tape over his mouth. Then Rangit rolled the man out of the trunk and half dragged him to the dumpster. He stood him up with difficulty and finally got him up enough to heave him over the side into the dumpster. He fell heavily into the cardboard trash and plastic bags of waste in the dumpster.

Rangit drove onto the terminal access road and, in time, rejoined the waiting taxicabs at the terminal. After he had been there a half hour, since he did not hear from Lero or Jean, he got out his handheld transceiver and connected the lead from his rooftop taxi cab radio antenna to the handheld. He held it below his chin so it would not be observed by passers by and chose a frequency.

"High Pockets, this is Jockey. Deuce is doing well. Message 19. Do you have a story for me?"

Translated, this meant: "Poseidon, this is Rangit. The pair of operatives you sent are proceeding with the mission without any interference so far. Message 19 meant that Lero or Jean would contact them when able. Do you have instructions for me?"

The transceiver was silent for a minute or longer, then Rangit heard: "Thanks, Jockey. Messages 26 and 31. Thanks."

Rangit knew that Message 26 was "Report received and acknowledged. Stand by." Message 31 meant: "Remain in area if possible."

He shut off the transceiver and pretended to take a nap in the driver's seat while he waited for a fare. It was 3:10 AM, and in a lull of airport activity, so he probably would not be disturbed for a while.

"Admiral Staker, we are ready with the on-line tele-conference," said Captain Overley.

"Very well," said Staker. Who took his seat at the conference table. The screen on the wall displayed the three other participants in the call: Harley Burger at CIA Special Ops, General Behm at NSA and the President.

Each man nodded to someone off camera before speaking. Then Staker spoke: "Mr. President, we want to bring you up to date with what we know at present. I will go first. Approximately an hour ago, your man Lero and his companion, Jean, landed at Karachi airport in an Air India Flight. They de-planed, picked up their luggage and got in the taxicab with Jockey, one of our assets in Karachi. Jockey is a native and very familiar with the area. The three of them used a ruse about picking up an aircraft that had been in the hangar for maintenance to trick the guard at the west door. Using an anesthetic dart, they captured him. Lero and Jean entered the hangar and left instructions with Jockey to wait for half an hour and if they were not outside by then, to contact Jefe and report. Jockey waited the time and Lero and Jean did not exit the hangar. We have not heard from them yet. Our belief at this time is that we should prepare for the probability that the captors of that aircraft will try to use it in some sort of terrorist strike. The aircraft has a fully fueled range of over eight thousand statute miles, so it could fly to our eastern states without refueling. We must not discount the possibility that they plan to strike Great Britain, either. We think we need to be ready to shoot the plane down over water, preferably over the English Channel if the aircraft heads for Great Britain, and over the Atlantic if the plane heads for the U.S. I will let Harley Burger speak next."

"Mr. President," said Burger, "We feel that, since we do not know the nationality or the identity of the people or group that has the aircraft, we need to plan for all contingencies. In the present circumstances, we agree that the strong probability is that the group is a Muslim extremist group and they intend to hit the U.S. However, we cannot discount the possibility that the group is Chechens who may be planning on hitting Moscow. This would achieve two purposes for them. It would devastate the Russians and would probably set off their retaliatory strikes toward the United States. If that happens, we will need to muster all of our missile countermeasures even though the Russians would be mistaken in striking at us. We will have to protect ourselves even though they think it is us that have hit them, when it is not. Another very minor probability is that the group that has the plane is a Nationalist Pakistani group that plans to hit India to once and for all get the Indians out of Kashmir. We believe that such a strike would be foolish and would result in essentially the destruction of Pakistan by the Indian military, but, as I said, we count this as a very minor improbable possibility."

The President asked: "General Behm, what can you add to the information we already have on the table?"

General Behm said: "Mr. President, our sources of all types tell us that the airplane is being repainted, but we do not know the livery or pattern they will use. Several large trucks have been observed

164

approaching the hangar in the last few hours. We believe that one of the convoys delivered three nuclear weapons, probably regional weapons from Chechnya, to the hangar and these are, indeed, loaded onto the aircraft. We also believe that the other trucks delivered about eighty drums of chemical and/or biological agents which have also been stowed on board. Those trucks came overland from Syria and arrived about two hours after the nukes were delivered. Obviously this plot has far reaching participation and planning."

"Thank you, General Behm," said the President. "General Staker, what measures do you recommend?

"Sir, I recommend that we put our Atlantic Fleet on full alert, including all of our nuclear submarines. All ships in the Mediterranean should be put on alert, also. We will alert all the ships and assets we have in the Persian Gulf and at Prince Sultan Airport in Saudi Arabia. We simply need every set of eyes we have standing by to pursue and down that aircraft. We have an aircraft carrier group in the Arabian Sea about two hundred nautical miles south west of Karachi and several ships in the area. As soon as the plane takes off, we will track it and once we are satisfied that it can be downed over water, we will shoot it down. If it heads for Moscow, we will hope it crosses over the Black Sea. If it heads for India somewhere, we may not be able to down it over water, but we will make that decision when and if we need to."

"Thank you, gentlemen. Sounds like you have your focus directed where it needs to be directed. Proceed as you outlined and keep me advised when you are able."

"Very well, Mr. President. Signing off," said Staker.

Chapter 35

Captain Turnage spoke to his Exec in the CIC of the Nimitz.

"Karl, put the ship on alert. We have a situation. I want two fighters, fueled and armed on the catapults as soon as you can. Put all the fighter and attack pilots on alert and set up a briefing for them in their ready room right away."

"Yes, sir," said Commander Charles and turned away to start getting that done.

Commander Ferrell of the Air Wing, keyed his microphone which was connected to the public address system in the hangar deck, the pilot's lounges, the sleeping quarters, and the briefing rooms.

"All pilots, all pilots, this is Commander Ferrell. Briefing in the pilots briefing rooms in fifteen minutes, that is twelve thirty local time. All pilots."

He raised his thumb from the switch button of the microphone and looked at the chart on the wall. It showed the ship was one hundred eighty nautical south southwest of Karachi. He started making notes for his briefing.

Commander Ferrell entered the briefing room from the rear, as is customary. The men out of courtesy, stood until he reached the podium. Then he put them "at ease" and they sat. The charts he had sent ahead were on the wall, but covered. This discouraged the men from ogling the charts rather than paying attention to what he was saying.

"Men, we have a situation. A group, the affiliation of which, we do not know, has hijacked a Boeing 777 and has flown it to a hangar in Karachi, under cover of night. It is being repainted in the hangar and loaded with weapons. We have reason to believe that they have three nukes on board, as well as numerous drums of chemical and/or biological weapons. This aircraft, when fully fueled, has a range of over seven thousand five hundred nautical miles. This means that it could hit, of course, any capital in Europe as well as any target east of the Mississippi in the U.S.. It could easily reach Moscow or Calcutta or Mumbai. At this time, we do not know what their intentions are. Our intel people believe the probability is high that they will try to cross the Atlantic and hit a target on our east coast. Since we must assume that they will persuade or coerce the Pakistani authorities to allow the plane to take off just like a normal air freight or passenger flight, in the middle of the night, not many people are watching. However, our people are watching. Your job, if it becomes necessary, is to shoot this plane down over open water. We have airborne eyes on this situation and our satellites are watching, too. We believe that they think they have gotten away with this so far and that they don't know that we know the plane's whereabouts.

This is a full court press, gentlemen. Every carrier, aircraft, missile destroyer, frigate, and submarine under our control is on full alert. Our satellite people and aerial observation people are working feverishly to watch what is going on. We know where they are now, but once they move, we have to be fluid and fast. If they go toward England, the plan is to splash this plane in the English Channel. If they go out over the Med, we will probably wait until it is over the Atlantic to act. The key is not to lose contact with this aircraft after it leaves Karachi. The traffic over Europe is light, compared to our own U.S. air traffic, but it bunches up over hubs like London and Amsterdam and Frankfort.

We will give you our best intel before you take off and update information as you pursue this aircraft. You may or may not be called upon because of distance from Karachi or direction, but if you are called on, we want you to be well rested and ready to fly. If you are called upon, it may involve aerial refueling and landing at a strange airport after your mission is completed. Fill your bags with charts for anything in the area from Mumbai on the east to the east coast of the U.S..

This first chart will give you an idea of the directions and distances to possible targets. It is also possible that they will fly over the pole to try to strike us. It will be very touchy for you to pursue this aircraft over Russia. We do not intend to alert the Russians that about this aircraft unless we have to. Our intel people think there is a small chance that the people in control are Chechen rebels and they intend to hit Moscow. If they do, the Russians may retaliate against us in the mistaken belief that we are responsible for the attack, thus the Chechens might get two objectives with one strike, so to speak.

Commanders will divide the air squadron into three groups. We will be on full alert, but each eight hours one group will be first in line. I don't need to tell you that this is very serious business. Give it your best effort. Thank you. That is all."

Similar briefings were being held on the carriers in the Atlantic and on the missile subs from Polyarny Inlet to south of Bermuda. All the electronic and human eyes that could be mustered, were looking. Until the group in the hangar made its move, they would just have to wait. It was thought that if they tried to storm the hangar, the terrorists would detonate the nukes, which would kill many millions of people.

Chapter 36

Admiral J. C. Kingery, the Director of the National Reconnaissance Office was on the line, calling General Behm at N.S.A.

"Jonah, I need to bring you up to date with this airplane situation," he said.

"OK," Jim, what can you tell me?" answered Kingery.

"As you know, our observation satellites can be aimed within an arc of about twenty degrees. As they pass over the area in question, they can give us and 'eyes on" look at that hangar for about twenty minutes of each hour. The rest of the time, we have to depend on our geosynchronous satellites, and, of course, there is the problem of cloud cover. South Asia is going to be socked in with low clouds beginning this morning for about thirty six hours. This situation puts us in a position of not being very able to give you reliable intel for a while. I know the situation is critical, but I wanted you to know our limitations so you won't be depending on us for intel when we cannot deliver. If the cloud cover dissipates, I will have our people let your people know. Sorry I can't give you any better news."

"Thanks," said Admiral Kingery. "We have to react to facts here. This is very touchy. We have to be in a position to notify the Russians and the British if we suspect that the aircraft is going toward them, but otherwise, the less said, the better. We have reason to believe that they have as many as three medium yield nukes on board, as well as up to fifty drums of chemical and/or biological agent. Even if we could take the aircraft where it is, disposing of the nukes and the chemical or bio agents would be a very touchy business. And, there is the matter of Pakistani sovereignty, too. We don't know if they are in on this or a potential victim. I would hate to turn this whole situation over to them in the open. Please keep me up to date and I will have my people keep you and yours as up to date as is prudent."

"Very well, thanks, Jim." The line disconnected.

It had been a long stressful day for the President. When he finally got to go to the residential quarters, he was tired, of course, but keyed up from the activities of the day and the stress. He decided to take a shower. He was thankful for the shower stall that President Johnson had had installed. President Johnson had complained that there was not enough water pressure, so the maintenance people had put a boost pump above the shower stall to raise the pressure. It was one of those doorless showers that one entered in a curving opening that eventually let one to the shower stall. I was fitted with a tiled bench where one could sit and let the steaming water bounce off. He had adjusted the water temperature and stepped into the stream and felt the luxurious warmth of the stream. He was not focusing on anything in particular with his eyes, but his mind was half a world away, thinking about Lero and Jean and the danger they were in. In his concentration, he failed to see or sense the arrival of the First Lady. She put her arm around his waist and pulled herself against his back. He sucked in a short breath of surprise and then instantly knew her touch. Liza was a southern girl and they had met when Fred was a young assistant to her father in Greenwood. They knew right away that they were drawn to each other. Now that the kids were off in college, they were empty nesters, so they had the residential quarters to themselves. Liza enjoyed having a nice tan, so she spent time around the pool at the secret residence they maintained in Virginia horse country, about an hour from the White House. He had not noticed that she was "home" when he strode through and undressed on his way to the shower. Now, here she was, with both wet arms wrapped around him. He did not turn around, but reached back around her to stroke her back and other features.

"The thing I miss the most about your being President is the scarcity of time we get to ourselves. I know it is necessary, but I am so glad we have some privacy here in the residence. But, I will tell you that, even when we are in bed, I don't feel private enough. This is the only place where I feel we are truly alone."

She let up a little on her grasp around his waist, so he could turn and face her.

"You are so beautiful in this light," he said. "I am so grateful for you."

He reached around her waist, which by now was wet with water and soap suds. He loved the way her waist felt to his arm and the way the front of her felt smashed against him. She reached up and put her arms around his neck and pulled herself up against him, and kissed him with all the feeling that she had stored up since the last time. With his arms around her waist, she felt safe to wrap her legs around him. All soapy and warm, they joined. It was a special moment together, that made the stresses of the day go away and made them appreciate each other for the comfort they gave each other.

(Since we are discussing an intimate moment between the President and the First Lady, out of respect for the office and for them personally, we will go into no further detail here, but suffice it to say that it was one of their most unforgettable moments of his first term.)

As she toweled off, he brought her a snuggly terry cloth robe and draped it over her water spattered back.

"If you don't mind, I think I will leave it here in the bathroom. I can get it later," she said.

174

"I don't mind a bit," he said, as he gratefully followed her into the bedroom.

Chapter 37

In the aft cargo hold, Pyotr and Alexi waited
patiently in their separate drums. Each drum was
lashed to others on a pallet, but was on a corner of
the pallet. Each drum had been specially outfitted
with oxygen and the ability to open from the inside.
Each was padded and had room for each to sit
inside. It was cramped, but it was very effective.
Besides, they would only be in the drums until about
half an hour after take- off. Then they could open up
and take action. They both knew the plan. Each was
well armed with a pistol, a 9mm close quarters
assault rifle, smoke and anesthetic grenades, nylon
tie wraps, a hand held transceiver, food and water.
Now, it only was a matter of waiting until the best
time to strike. Then they could take over from the
Iranians and head for Moscow. In a merciful
gesture, their commandant had provided another
drum with parachutes and high altitude breathing
apparatus for each of them, so they could bail out
after they set the auto pilot and the timers.

Lieutenant Harold Brubaker gripped the dispatch
with left hand and with his right, removed the soggy
unlit cigar from his mouth. His mouth remained open
as he read the dispatch which had just been handed

to him on the bridge. Then he threw the cigar into the trash can beside him.

"FROM: RAMPARTS (Commander Fifth Fleet, USN)
TO: LT H Brubaker, Commander, (guided Missile Frigate) Reuben James:

Go to and remain at FULL ALERT, DEFCON Three immediately. Report ready or not ASAP by satellite link. Maintain security in all radio transmissions by using scrambler. Assure that all missiles in the cans are hot and ready to go. Assure that duty personnel and their relief persons are alerted to possible missile launch. Unable to predict the timing of the threat, possibly several hours. Will warn of eminent danger based on intel as soon as possible. Maintain ready status until stood down by RAMPARTS. Acknowledge.

"Chief," said Brubaker, "Light up the PA system and hand me the mike."

The chief did as ordered and handed the Lieutenant the mike.

"All hands, this is the Captain. Pursuant to order from Commander, Fifth Fleet, we are at GENERAL QUARTERS and will remain so until further order. Possible threat message from Fleet advises that we need to remain on alert for a number of hours and may have to act on short notice. All ordnance men, make sure that the missiles in the cans are hot and

ready. Back up crews be alert to a call to action.
THIS IS NO DRILL."

He switched off the microphone by raising his thumb
and handed the mike back to the chief.

"I wonder what the hell is going on," he thought to
himself.

"Chief, tell the corpsman that I will take meals here
on the bridge until further notice and ask him to
bring me a pot of coffee."

"Yes sir, said the chief and complied.

Lieutenant Brubaker looked at the plot next to the
compass. It showed their position about three
hundred nautical west south west of the English
coast. The ship continued to maintain position in the
shallow swells. The sky was overcast and the night
was very dark. The ship's complement did not
notice the darkness of the night, except for those on
the bridge.

"Chief, send a coded message to RAMPARTS. Say
that Reuben James is at DEFCON Three and will
remain so until relieved or stood down."

"Yes, sir," said the chief and the antenna near the
top of the mast sent the message to the satellite in a
burst transmission.

Chapter 38

Colonel Gori's cell phone rang.

"Grandfather, greetings," the voice said.

"And the same to you, Sergei. How is your mother doing?"

"Both she and papa are doing well and are comfortable," said the voice.

"Please continue to inform me how they are doing, Sergei," said the Colonel.

"I will, grandfather. I need to ring off now, they are calling my flight."

"Very well. Thanks again, Sergei." The line went silent.

What sounded like a family update on the health status of two relatives, in fact, told Colonel Gori that the two agents succeeded in staying behind in the airplane and were in the specially equipped drums, waiting to act.

Gori tapped on the glass partition in the Zlin limousine and the driver motored off slowly into the cold night.

"It won't be long now," thought Gori.

Chapter 39

The ornate telephone rang beside the bed in the Chairman's personal quarters.

"Chairman Yishenko, I need to speak to you," said General Zeltkin.

"Can it now wait until tomorrow morning?" asked Chairman Yeshenko.

Yeshenko wanted to stay in his warm bed with Mirina his mistress. She had just removed her peignoir that he had gotten her in Paris the month before and was approaching him as Yeshenko spoke to Zeltkin. A mocking pout came across her face as she realized that his responsibilities would take him away for at least a part of their night together.

Yeshenko tossed the covers off of his nude body and tried to go to the stand that held his clothes. She pressed herself against him and playfully asked how long he might be gone.

"I will just be a short while. General Zeltkin has something that is very important to tell me. I need to meet him in the secure room."

He raised her right breast with his left hand and tenderly kissed her lips and neck. Then, with a quick pat on her rump, he quickly walked to the stand and dressed himself. In thirty seconds, he was out the door and walking hastily down the hall.

As he approached the secure room, the armed guard came to attention and, when he was about ten feet away, swung the heavy door open for Yeshenko. General Zeltkin was already inside, pacing back and forth. When he saw Yeshenko, he approached so they could whisper to each other. Even though both of the men had been told that the room was secure, they still exercised extreme caution when addressing matters of high sensitivity. This was one of those moments.

"Yosef, we have discovered that the ISI has hijacked a Boeing 777 aircraft from Maylasian Airlines. It was on a flight from Kuala Lumpur to Peking and disappeared from radar about a half hour after take-off. We discovered the aircraft in flight and tracked it to Karachi. It is now in a hangar being repainted. What really alarms me is that our sources inform me that Colonel Gori of the NKVD took three nuclear weapons from the storage depot in Tiblisi last night about eleven PM local time. The weapons were put onto large military trucks and disappeared shortly after that. The last pass of our surveillance satellite over Karachi spotted some heavy trucks of about the same capacity northbound north of the Karachi airport. We believe that the trucks are returning after delivering the weapons to the hangar in Karachi. We do not have any assets within visual range of the hangar, but we suspect that Colonel Gori is either trying to put together a terrorist attack with the ISI agents, or may be acting on his own on behalf of the Chechen resistance and the ISI people do not know it. I recommend that we quietly alert General Makarov of the Air Force to alert enough pilots to take action against the airliner if they indeed to intend to strike us rather than the United States."

"Karl, that is good work," said Yeshenko. "Alert the General in charge of the air forces in that area, but tell him to keep this quiet. Keep a tight rein on intel and let me know immediately if there is any activity."

"Thank you, Chairman. I will do as you order. May I reach you on the same number as before?"

"Yes," said Yeshenko. "Call me with any news. This was good work, Karl."

Yeshenko patted the General on the shoulder as they exited the secure room. Then he walked quickly back up the long vaulted hallway to his quarters.

Chapter 40

Almost at the same moment, the phone rang in the British Prime Minister's residence. An aide answered. "May I help you?"

The voice on the phone said: "Mister Murfree is calling to speak to Magi."

"Just a moment, please," said the aide and put the phone down.

He went a few feet and tapped quietly on the door. A quiet voice inside said, "Yes."

The aide stuck his head inside the door opening and said to the Prime Minister, "It is the President of the United States, calling you on the secure line."

The Prime Minister carefully pulled his arm from beneath the waist of his wife. Her satin nightgown made it easier to slip his pajama clad arm out from under her.

He quickly put on his robe and tied the sash as he went out the door quietly.

The aide handed him the secure phone.

"This is Magi," he said.

Magi this is Murfree, say the word.

The Prime Minister said softly into the phone "Corona."

The President then said "Aurora," and they both then knew that they were, indeed, speaking to the intended party.

"Mr. Prime Minister, excuse the interruption in the middle of the night, but we have a situation."

"Not to worry, what is the problem?" asked Nigel Browne, the Prime Minister.

"That Malaysian airliner that disappeared has been hijacked. The hijackers flew it out of radar contact to Karachi where it is now being refitted and repainted. We anticipate a terror strike, but we do not know their intended target. I want to keep this as quiet as possible. If the terrorists who have the aircraft think they have been detected, they may detonate the three nuclear weapons we believe they have on board. Our analysts believe, based on who we believe has the airplane, that they intend to fly it across the Atlantic and hit us somewhere on our eastern seaboard. We think that there is a slight chance that they will try to hit your country, but the second most likely target, our analysts believe, is Moscow. There are Chechen rebels involved with the ISI in this. They took three medium power nuclear weapons from a KGB warehouse in Tiblisi yesterday and have trucked or otherwise transported them to Karachi. If the Russians get hit, they may incorrectly assume that we did it and they may retaliate on a broad scale, possibly even launching a few ICBMs at your country. I will leave it to you how broadly you want to alert your military people, but we have every asset between Calcutta and Chicago on full alert. If they start out over the Atlantic, we intend to splash the aircraft in deep water, but if they appear to be heading toward you, we would like your advice about what action you want us to take or what you will do yourself."

"Thank you for alerting me, Mr. President. I will keep this quiet, but will alert our forces just in case. Please keep me informed of developments."

"I will, Mr. Prime Minister, and thank you.

"Fred, I wish you would call me Nigel."

"OK, Nigel. Get some rest. I have a feeling tomorrow is going to be a pip."

"Will do, Fred. Good night."

Chapter 41

Major Rawal met with Captain Ahmed and Captain Dissi and the four officers who would take turns piloting the plane to its destination. All preparations had been made. The plane was fully fueled and all systems checked. The bodies and baggage had been removed and were on their way to a watery grave in the Indian Ocean. The plane had been repainted over the original livery of Malaysian Airlines to now show it belonged to Federal Express, an American company. The nuclear devices were on board and secured. The chemical and biological agents were on board, likewise secured. The pilots had their charts and food and drink for the trip. The pilots, civilian airline pilots, two from Iran Air and two from Air Pakistan, stood ready. Now was the moment of greatest tension. When they called Jinnah Clearance Delivery to ask for their clearance and permission to start and taxi, their plan was put to its ultimate test. If they could just take off, they felt that anyone who might have discovered their plot would be afraid to take action against the plane over any land mass over which it might fly on its way westward. If they could slip through the airspace between here and Paris on the bogus Federal Express flight plan, they could achieve their objective. As one last detail of their preparations, they all put out their prayer rugs and bowed toward Mecca and worshipped together in the darkened office of the hangar manager.

Then they exchanged embraces and good wishes. Then the critical moment arrived. The pilots walked into the doorway of the Boeing and went forward to the flight deck. The ship was ghostly quiet without electricity and the two hundred fifty eight souls that had died in it. They had earlier drawn lots to see which two would make the departure flight and fly the first leg of six hours. Captains Musala and Pindi went through all the system check outs and decided the aircraft was ready to start. Now they needed the big doors on the end of the hangar opened so the tug could pull the giant aircraft out onto the tarmac for start-up. It was still completely dark when Musala, using a hand held radio to keep from having to turn on the master switch of the 777, radioed the ground crew and told the driver of the tug that they were ready to be towed out. The driver acknowledged with a hand signal and started his tug. Just like it was any other ordinary departure, the driver pulled the 777 out of the hangar onto the tarmac and turned it ninety degrees to the left so it could taxi onto a taxiway for the runways. Now the critical moment arrived. Captain Pindi, from the first officer's seat, the right seat, his face sweaty with fear, keyed the mike of the handheld and broadcast: "Jinnah Clearance Delivery, Federal Express three fourteen, at the Ispahani Hangar ready to pick up our clearance for Paris and engine start in ten minutes."

"Federal Express Three Fourteen, stand by," said the controller. Long seconds passed. Beads of sweat rolled down the faces and chests of the pilots. This was the critical moment.

Then the controller keyed his mike and said: "Federal Express three fourteen, you are cleared to Charles Degaulle at Paris via jet route 6, expect twenty four thousand feet ten minutes after departure, contact ground on one two five decimal seven. Good morning."

Pindi breathed for the first time in a minute, it seemed. He shook as he keyed his mike and said: "Roger, clearance, Fed Ex three fourteen, cleared to Charles De Gaulle via jet route 6, expect twenty four thousand ten after take off, over to ground on point seven."

"Readback correct, three fourteen. Have a good flight."

Something could still go wrong, but Pindi turned the dial of the transceiver and called ground control.

"Jinnah Ground, Fed Ex three fourteen at the Ispanhani hangar, with information India, ready to start engines and taxi."

"Roger, Fed Ex three fourteen, Jinnah ground, cleared for engine start, when ready, taxi to runway Seven Right by way of taxiways Juliet and November. Hold short of Runway Seven Left."

"Roger, Jinnah Ground, Fed Ex Three fourteen starting engines and will taxi to Runway Seven right via taxiways Juliet and November, hold short of Runway Seven Left. Thank you."

Pindi gave a thumbs up signal to the ground crew manning the start cart and began to read off the start-up check list for Captain Musala. They were both covered with sweat. Soon, though, the air conditioning system kicked on and the flight deck began to cool off.

When all the engines had been started and all gauges checked and the check list gone through and all challenges had been satisfactorily answered, Captain Musala said: "Brake release. Here we go."

The landing lights of the mammoth plane bathed the taxiways with white light. They wove their way from the tarmac in front of the Ispahani hangar onto Taxiway Juliet. Then, two hundred yards further, turned onto Taxiway November which led to the active Runways. Because they had to cross Runway Seven Left in order to get to Seven Right, they stopped at the "hold" line on the taxiway and called the tower, as instructed.

"Jinnah Tower, Federal Express Three Fourteen requesting permission to cross Runway Seven Left and proceed to Seven Right."

"Roger, Fed Ex Three fourteen, hold short for arriving DC-10 traffic on two mile final."

"Roger," said Musala, "Three fourteen holding short."

Both pilots watched the big DC-10 come down final. In about forty seconds, it passed in front of them and touched down with a cloud of burned rubber and scrubbing tires, its landing gear struts accepting the weight of the great aircraft as it rolled down the runway.

About ten second later, the tower called.

"Fed Ex three fourteen, cross Runway Seven Left, taxi into position and hold on Seven right."

"Roger," said Musala, "Three fourteen position and hold on Seven right."

Once again, sweat beaded up on Musala and Pindi as they waited for take-off clearance. They both knew that this might be their last take off. They also knew that there many ways in which this whole thing could go wrong, but they were committed. Hundreds of people had worked for a long time to get them to this moment. Now, they would show the Great Satan that they could strike at its heart.

"Fed Ex Three fourteen, cleared to take off, Runway Seven right. Fly runway heading, contact departure on one two five decimal three on departure. Have a good flight."

Roger, three fourteen. We are rolling."

Musala and Pindi looked at each other with a look of relief and cautious joy. They smiled and placed their hands on the power levers and gradually brought them forward to their stops. The great plane came alive and began its takeoff roll. Eighteen seconds later, Three fourteen lifted its nose wheels and arched into the night.

Now Musala and Pindi were so busy with flying that they were distracted from their relief at being released to take off and leave Jinnah Airport. The black night ahead seemed a welcome sight as they went through the after take-off check list.

Chapter 42

In the commissary compartment, Lero and Jean waited approximately thirty minutes after they felt the airplane take off. There was no way in their windowless compartment that they could tell what direction the airplane was flying. In any case, it was time to act.

They double checked their weapons and extra magazines. Each had a black head cover to pull over their heads, revealing only their eyes. It was as much for concealment and stealth as protection from a sudden temperature drop.

As they finished, Lero took Jean by the arm. He said: "I just want you to know that this last year and a half have been the happiest time of my life. I am so sorry to get you into this. This is a very dangerous situation. If we can get control of the aircraft, we will contact our people and follow their orders about what to do. If we cannot gain control, we may detonate our grenades to cause the airplane to crash. Remember that this is war. We have to assume that anyone on the airplane is an enemy. Do not hesitate to use lethal force. Our goal is to breech the cockpit and take over from those in control. Be on guard the moment we open this hatch. We have no way of knowing how many people are on board. Conserve your ammunition. Are you ready?"

Jean gave a solemn nod. He had double checked her assault rifle and its extra magazines. He knew from their practice sessions that she was a very good shot and could handle the assault rifle as well as anyone.

Lero opened the aluminum hatch as quietly as he could. The noise of the airstream and the engines created enough noise that they need not worry about small noises. The commissary compartment opened into a luggage hold, which they determined was empty. With only their flashlights for illumination, they crossed the diamond patterned floor boards to the far exit. Between that compartment and the next, there was a ladder next to the elevator into the galley between the first class compartment and the tourist section. There was room in the elevator for only one of them, so Lero would go up first.

They went past the pallets of drums secured to the floor with ratchet belt devices. The markings on the drums were in Urdu, saying that they had been manufactured in Iraq in the 1980s. Lero and Jean continued rearward to search the entire ship before they attempted to breach the flight deck. Just as they got to the hatch at the end of the cargo compartment, one of the drums opened. The man who stuck his head out did not see them immediately, but was just relieved to be getting out of the drum. Lero and Jean froze in the dark. The man got out of the drum and retrieved his weapon from inside and went away from them to the second pallet. He tapped on a drum on the corner and in a few seconds, the lid opened and a second man raised his head out of the drum. Because neither of them expected to encounter anyone in the cargo compartment, they did not look for Lero and Jean. Lero took Jean's arm and pointed her to go to the other side of the end of the cargo bay. He moved toward the corner nearest him, hoping that the men would either come toward them and he and Jean could down them, or they would go the other way, and he and Jean could wait to take them until later.

As luck would have it, the men came toward Lero and Jean. As they got about fifty feet away, they spotted Jean and raised their weapons. They and Jean fired at the same time. Jean's rounds hit one square in the chest and he fell backwards onto the deck. At the same time, Jean gave a groan and was knocked backwards and fell heavily on the deck.

By this time, Lero had moved toward the front, so he could have a clear field of fire. He shot the second man with a short burst and he went down limply, his weapon scattering on the aluminum floor. Lero raced to the men and determined that both were dead, then he quickly went to Jean, expecting the worst. By the time he got to her, she was moving her arms and legs, so he knew she was alive. One of the man's rounds had hit a spare magazine that Jean had tucked into her tunic. The bullet caused the magazine to hit her flat in the chest, knocking the wind out of her. He looked her over quickly and found the magazine, smoking and bent where the round had hit it. She gave him a look like she did not realize what had happened. He held her up and made sure that there were no other wounds. He kissed her forehead and her cheek and hugged her.

"Are you OK?" he asked.

"FFFFine," she whispered. "It knocked the breath out of me. I am woozy. Give me a minute."

He cradled her shoulders and head next to him. Evidently, if there were anyone else on board outside of the flight deck, they were holding back.

"If there are any other people in the cargo hold, they certainly would have heard that exchange of fire. The people in the flight deck, may not have heard it, though, with all the wind noise and engine whine," he said. She nodded indicating she understood, but still spoke with difficulty.

"What now," she asked.

"I will put these bodies back into the drums and we will continue toward the front of the aircraft. Cover me while I do this. Can you do that?" he asked.

She was feeling better, and said, "If you will let me do that from a kneeling position, I think I will be OK.

I am recovering pretty well, but I still don't want to stand, if that is OK."

"Sure," he said. Just keep a close eye out for any more people. Shout to me if you see anyone."

She nodded and he went over to the first man and dragged him by the shoulders to the first drum. Before he tried to lift him to the lip of the drum, he searched his pockets to see if there were any identifying objects or documents on him. The man had been carrying an H & K nine millimeter assault rifle, made in Germany. He had no wallet and no identifying papers or money or objects that would give a clue, so Lero stood and bent over and picked the man up around the chest below the arms and lugged him up to the lip of the drum. He let the man down head first into the drum and reached down and got a hold of his legs and lifted them up to feed them down into the drum. The man folded the correct way and crumpled into the drum. Lero put the top back on and latched it. Then he went to the second man. Jean's rounds had hit him in the upper chest and one bullet had entered his neck in the middle. There was a good bit of blood on the deck and Lero avoided it so he would not slip. He dragged the man over to where he could get access to his pockets without getting blood on his soles and hands. There were no clues on the second man, either, but it was clear that they intended to take the aircraft with force, so Lero concluded that whoever had control of the aircraft were the targets of these two. He returned to where Jean was kneeling. She was feeling better now and stood as he approached.

"No clues on those guys. The assault rifles they carried were H & K nine millimeter. German make, like ours. Probably carried them to throw off identification. The look of these guys was European, not Arabic or Asian, so we can rule out Pakistanis and Orientals, but they could be from a lot of different places. I think they are not the same group that has control of the aircraft.

"Since we cannot contact anyone just now, and we cannot see anything outside, we have to get to window to see if we can determine anything about the direction of flight visually. I don't think we should wait too long to take on the guys in the flight deck. If they intend to hit Russia, they will be turning north, but my guess is they intend to hit the U.S. and will go west on a commercial airway to look like any other commercial passenger or freight flight. If we can find a good hiding place near the nose of the plane, we will be well placed to take over when the time comes."

He took her hand and they walked the long, dark cargo hold to its front.

Chapter 43

"Mr. President, it is General Behm," said the aide.

President Thompson took the telephone.

"What do you have, Harley?" asked the President.

"Sir, we have determined that the aircraft took off from Karachi about a half hour ago. It appears to be imitating a cargo flight from Karachi to Paris, using a Federal Express livery and N number. We don't know who requested the flight plan, but Fed Ex operations in Memphis received a telephone call from someone who identified himself to Jonesy and gave the data for the flight plan. Fed Ex ops filed the flight plan before we intercepted it. I have shared this information with CentCom, CIA and Fifth Fleet. Everybody is alerted."

"Thanks, Harley. Keep me advised. I will be up late tonight, so do not be reluctant to call later."

"Will do, Mr. President," and he rang off.

Chapter 44

Lero and Jean made their way, compartment by compartment, in the dark, using only their flashlights, to the compartment beneath the galley in the front section of the aircraft. There was an amber glow coming from an LED on the bulkhead. Jean discovered it was a light switch. She asked if it were OK to turn on the light. Lero said it was OK, so she tripped the switch. The fluorescent lights took a few seconds to come up, so they were not temporarily blinded. They found they were in a compartment that was about eight by ten feet and ten feet tall. There were lockers on every square foot of wall space. Some had dishes in them, some had coffee cups, some had condiments and there was a pair of freezers with meals ready to heat in the microwave for the passengers, who would now never see them. Jean turned to speak directly to Lero and she sucked her breath in and he could see the shock on her face.

There was a trickle of blood coming down his right temple. She said: "You are wounded. There is a trickle of blood. Here, let me have a look."

She took her flashlight and shined it on his head. There was a small neat hole in his pullover mask.

She helped him take off his mask, which he did. She did not need the flashlight to see the blood now. There was a puncture wound in his right temple, just above the hair line. A thin, but constant flow of blood was coming out.

"You have a bullet wound in your scalp. Do you feel anything there?" she asked.

"No, no pain or other unusual feelings. No numbness, either," he said.

"This is dangerous. This must have been a ricochet or something. Clearly if you had been hit by a round directly from that assault rifle at this range, it would have gone clear through your head," she said. "You seem fine now, but what if you are bleeding internally? You could have a subdural hematoma. Sometimes they can be symptom free for a long time and the symptoms can onset unexpectedly.

Lero said: "I don't need to tell you that I will need you to help me land this plane. We cannot depend on the people now in control to make a safe landing after we take over. They would deliberately crash the plane if they got a chance, and there may be millions of people below us that would be killed and Lord knows how many injured or sickened.   What do you think we should do?"

"This is not good, Jean. You are right. This may cause symptoms suddenly with no warning. I feel fine just now, vision clear, full manual dexterity, but clearly, the clock is running. I will need surgery for this, I know, but right now, we must take this aircraft while I can still help you."

They stood in silence for a few moments. Then Lero spoke again: "We will go up to the passenger compartment above us by using the elevator, one at a time. When the first one gets up there, there may be people to encounter. Obviously, we need to dispatch them before we assault the flight deck. If I am lost in a fire fight as soon as I get up there, do your best to dispatch those people and get into the cockpit if you can. Shoot the pilots if you have to, and put the plane on auto pilot. It probably is already on autopilot, but if not, engage it first, then call for help on the international distress frequency, 121.5 or 243. The guys will tell you what to do."

Jean shivered with fright. She was frightened about losing Lero. She was frightened about having to encounter the unknown number of highjackers above. She was frightened about having to control the airplane by herself and she was frightened about having to land a plane so huge without any training. She visibly shook and, after shaking, she seemed to be calmer and nodded to him that she was ready. They checked their weapons again, making sure that each had a full magazine in each weapon.

Jean helped Lero get into the elevator. With all his gear, it was a tight squeeze. After he got in, he said: "I think I ought to get out and peel off some of this gear. Mobility will be at a premium up there. I can always come back for the gear or get you to bring it up. Just give me the H & K and the extra magazines and let's leave the rest here for now."

Chapter 45

"General, we have found something," said Major Hooper to General Behm. "Our people have discovered that a bogus flight plan was filed by telephone from the Operations Desk at Federal Express. They said a man known to them called and gave them the information for the flight plan, but when they and we talked to the man, he said he did not know anything about it. Clearly, these people know how to operate within the air traffic system. We are still trying to use telephone data to find out who called and from where. I will keep you up to date."

"Get me General Binghampton at the Ops Center, please, said Behm.

Major Hooper took a moment at his desk, then punched in the numbers on his satellite phone. When the aide answered, he said: "General Behm to speak to General Binghampton, please." There was a delay of a few seconds and then Hooper said, "Right, hold please," and he nodded and handed the headset to Behm.

"Spike, we have a situation. I will go into detail later, but where are your F-117s in Europe or the Med (Mediterranean) just now?"

"We have six at Mendenhall, England, General."

"Good, we have a hijacked 777 off of Karachi, heading northwesterly. We don't know what the intended target is, but we are informed that they have three nukes on board and some chemical and/or biological weapons. We feel that the highest probability is that they intend to fly transatlantic and hit us somewhere on the eastern seaboard. We don't want to alert them or take any action against the plane as long as it is not an imminent threat, but we need to get Stealth fighters up and close to the plane in case we need to act over Europe. We need to keep our surveillance secret, so I thought the Stealth Fighters would be the best equipment to achieve that. The aircraft is now about five hundred nautical north west of Karachi. Can you scramble a flight to intercept and follow the plane and replace the planes periodically to keep the pilots fresh as the flight comes northwest over Europe? Can you get a KC-135 or KC-10 up over central Europe to refuel these guys if they have to loiter?"

'Yes, we can, General. We have KC-135s at Incerlik (U.S. Air Base in southern Turkey) from the Ohio National Guard and one KC-10. I can get their squadron on this right away. Just give me a minute to get this rolling and I will get back on the line with you."

He put the phone down.

"Colonel Jessup, alert Mendenhall, scramble a flight of two F-117s immediately, instruct them to fly southeast and we will radio them a flight plan and instructions in flight. Send them hot, with guns and missiles. Alert the Refueling Squadron at Incerlik that I need an immediate launch of a tanker over central Europe."

"Yes sir," said Jessup and turned to his work.

"General, the F-117s are scrambled and the tankers will be airborne shortly. We will update them with a flight plan as soon as our guys generate one."

"Good, General. Can you maintain radio contact with the fighters from your command post?"

"Yes, General, we have repeaters and will be in communications with them by satellite."

"I will have our intel people tell yours where the aircraft is just now. It is flying on a bogus FedEx flight plan. Keep me in touch with any developments, please."

"Will do, sir. Thanks for your confidence in us. Talk to you later."

Then Behm spoke to his aide, Major Hooper again as he handed him the headset:

"Thanks, Major Hooper. Good work. Keep me advised," said Behm.

Chapter 46

Colonel Gori looked at his watch. He knew that the 777 had taken off from Karachi at zero five twelve local time. The special mission watch he wore on his left wrist was set to Karachi, or, as he called it, Mission time. In the radar center in Vilnius, he watched on the computer screen where all commercial flights were depicted for the region. He could see several aircraft designators stretching out to the northwest from Karachi. He knew it had to be one of three aircraft displayed. Air traffic control for the Karachi area and any to the west would have the type of aircraft, the company or country of the aircraft, the flight or registration number and the altitude as well as the DME speed. Since he was using a commercially available program that showed commercial aircraft aloft without the air traffic control data, he could not tell which one, exactly was the 777 with his agents on board. He knew that people close to the Ayotullah would be watching the same thing he was watching. They fully expected the blip on their screens to track a course toward Charles De Gaulle airport in Paris, and then on to the west. Gori's plan was for his men to take the plane over about half an hour after departure and divert it toward Moscow. What he did not know was that his men were dead and the nukes he had so carefully stolen from the KGB were not on their way to Moscow. It would be any time in the next half hour that the aircraft would show a course diversion toward the north. He watched patiently, sipping a coffee with cream. No one else in the center knew what he was up to. They just assumed that he was making a security inspection or maybe just killing time until his flight back to Moscow.

"Your Supremacy, the pilots have departed Karachi and are using a bogus flight plan for Paris. We need only to watch as the aircraft progresses to Paris. Once in Paris air space, by the time it gets to Paris, our operatives will have filed an amended flight plan to take the aircraft to Philadelphia. If the aircraft can be slipped through the airspace above Paris, it will not likely have any problems getting to the United States. Once past radar coverage from Britain, it will be in a radar free environment like all other trans-Atlantic flights. It is a great triumph to get this far along without a hitch. May Allah be praised."

"Yes, yes," mumbled the Ayatollah and returned to his reading.

Chapter 47

The phone rang in the Situation Room at the White House. The President's Naval Aide, Admiral Boster, picked up the phone.

"Situation Room, Admiral Boster," he said. "Yes, just a moment."

"It is Admiral Staker, for you, sir," said Admiral Boster.

The President took the phone.

"Yes, Admiral," said the President.

"Sir, I asked our people to plot the expected flight path of the subject aircraft on its flight to Paris. We thought we should determine if there were a suitable place to down the aircraft to achieve minimal casualties on the ground. The flight path will not take the aircraft over any significant body of water. Our technical people, using the intel that we have that there are three medium yield nuclear devices on board, have calculated that at detonation, if the aircraft is at an optimal altitude of one thousand feet above ground level, there will be complete devastation over an area with a diameter of ten miles and substantial structural damage for another ten miles out. Casualties will vary with the population density of the area struck, but it could be in the millions if the devices are detonated over a major population area. Our suggestion now is just to wait. If they have technicians aboard, they might detonate the devices if we try to force the plane to land or shoot it down. Our advice at this time is to stand by for an opportunity to shoot the aircraft down, and if it continues past Paris out over the Atlantic, we will have plenty of time and opportunity to shoot it down."

The President replied, "Thanks. But this puts us in another spot. If we alert the French, they may try to shoot the aircraft down before it enters their airspace. This could degenerate into the proverbial game of "hot potato." Very dangerous. Of course, this line of thought is offset by the desire to help our allies any way we can. We have to keep in mind that they have the right to defend their sovereign territory and it will be many hours before the aircraft can threaten the United States territory. Let's plan a launch of fighter jets on short notice all along the route to intercept and shoot the aircraft down if necessary. I don't want anyone tailing the aircraft for fear that the people responsible have others watching on radar for such a move on our part."

"I will see to it, Mr. President. I don't envy you this responsibility. Please call on us if we can help you in any way. We will continue to update you when things change," said Admiral Staker.

"Thanks. Talk to you later," said the President, and gave the headset to the aide to hang it up.

"Get me Prime Minister Avia, please," he said to the aide.

In a few moments, the aide handed him the headset again, and nodded.

"Hello," said the President.

"Hello, Mr. President," said Prime Minister Avia. "To what do I owe the honor of this call," he said.

"There is a dire situation that I need to let you know about. Some group has hijacked a Boeing 777 and loaded it with what we believe is three nuclear devices and perhaps some chemical and/or biological weapons. It departed Karachi about an hour ago, ostensibly on a bogus flight plan for Paris. We believe at this time that the greatest probability is that they intend to fly the plant across the Atlantic and strike us somewhere on our east coast. Because our people believe that there is a slight chance that they intend to strike Israel, I wanted to let you know. We will be watching this flight very carefully, as you might expect. If it so much as twitches in a southerly direction, we will take action against it to protect you. We will notify you immediately if such a diversion occurs so you can alert your people, but we thought your military and intelligence people should be alerted at this time.

We are reluctant to take action against the aircraft at present because of the danger to people on the ground beneath its flight path. Our intent is to down the aircraft once it is a safe distance out in the Atlantic."

"My goodness, Mr. President. What a dangerous situation. Thank you so much for alerting me. I will put our people quietly but quickly on alert. Please call me immediately if there is the change in course you mentioned. We will depend on your radar and satellite observations and would appreciate periodic updates. Again, thank you , Mr. President."

"You are welcome, Rudi. I will keep you up to date. It would not hurt to pray a little about this."

"I will, Mr. President. Good luck. Talk to you later." The line went silent.

Chapter 48

Colonel Gori dialed a number on his satellite telephone. The voice on the other end just answered: "Da." (Yes.)

In Russian, Colonel Gori said: "Whaling can be risky this time of the year."

The voice on the other end said, "I prefer walrus, myself." Then Colonel Gori knew that he was talking to Colonel Petcovich of the KGB.

"There is a problem. I have not heard from our men. The time when they were supposed to act has come and gone. I think we should energize the alternate plan. If, before it can reach the travelers, we do hear from our men, we can call it off and let the original plan play out," said Gori.

"Sometimes so much depends on so few people. If the golden goose does not produce, we will lose the entire opportunity. A banquet for unexpected guests may be the only alternative. However, if the first team is still in charge, we could let them stay in the game for the second half. So many of our people have died under tyrants in the last hundred years, it seems a shame not to be able to set them free and start over," said Petcovich.

"Perhaps if the goose reaches its intended nesting ground, the reverse of the action expected from the first alternative will eventuate," said Gori. "We have done our best, Yuri. I am undecided what to do. What do you recommend?"

"I would rather let the goose go. I have no particular gripe with the alternate people. At least if the goose reaches its nest, we will have changed the ballgame."

"When do we have to act, Georgi?" asked Petcovich.

"We have a little less than two hours to act, but if we are going to the alternate plan, I need to herd the chickens in the next hour. Think about these things, Yuri and call me back."

"Will do," said Petcovich and hung up.

Chapter 49

Major Kuhns of the Intercept Department came in, all flustered and sweaty.

"General Behm, we just intercepted this satellite telephone call. Our voice recognition program says with a ninety nine percent probability the voice of one of the men in the call is Colonel Gori of the KGB. Thought you would want to hear this, sir."

"Yes, good work, Karl, play the conversation on the speaker so we can all hear it."

No one made a sound as the tape played in the speakers of the NSA Situation Room.

"Of course, they are talking in code, but what do you make of it, sir," asked Kuhns. "Could they be talking about the plane in Karachi?"

"Sure sounds like it, doesn't it? It would seem that they expected something to happen that did not happen and now they are pondering whether to go to an alternate plan or just let the plane fly on in control of the original crew," said Behm. "Make several copies of this tape, please and distribute it so that it will not be lost. Tell your technicians that this was an important catch, Karl. Thanks again."

Major Kuhns saluted with beaming pride, turned on his heel and left the Situation Room.

General Behm watched the small airplane symbol as it slowly moved across the map projected on the wall screen.

"This is a fine kettle of fish," he thought. "If we shoot this plane down over Europe or Britain, there could be millions of casualties and untold property damage. If we do nothing, the captors may do that themselves. On the other hand, if they do not crash the plane or detonate the devices and fly on over the Atlantic, we can shoot the plane down over deep water and prevent damage to the homeland. We are just going to have to wait these next three hours or so to see what they do, if anything. We need to alert NATO to the threat because the countries under threat need to take action to harden themselves against the possible damage. Even a detonation at high altitude would knock out the electrical grid and all the computers below which would cause havoc."

Chapter 50

As Colonel Gori stepped out of the radar control center, a military officer standing beside a large command car, turned and spoke to him.

"Colonel Gori?" he asked.

"Yes, I am Colonel Gori," was his response.

"I am Major Lashinsky, from NKVD. I have orders to place you under arrest," as he drew his pistol and held it down by his side.

A soldier got out of the right front seat of the command car, and receiving a nod from Lashinsky, came over and patted the Colonel down, searching for a weapon. Finding none, he nodded to the Major.

"Upon whose authority are you arresting me?" asked Gori.

"On the highest authority, Colonel. Take a seat in the car, please."

Gori reluctantly stepped forward and entered the car by the door being held by the soldier.

As the command car motored away, Colonel Gori thought of the gulags that he had visited as an officer. Now he might be a prisoner in one. Then he wondered if he would live to do so. He thought about the money he had salted away in the Caymans and wondered if it would buy his freedom.

Chapter 51

General Behm rubbed his chin in study for a few moments. Then he spoke to his aide: "Get me Admiral Donnaker, please."

The aide immediately signaled to the chief petty officer that he needed to place a call and the chief took down the directions. In less than thirty seconds, the aide handed General Behm the headset, with a nod.

"Jack, this is Daryl. Are you advised about the airplane from Karachi?"

"Yes, Jack. What do you want me to do?"

"I want you to get a fighter up there, close enough to the plane so as not to show up on anybody's radar as a separate aircraft. We need to be able to splash that airplane on a few minutes' notice. There was evidently some sort of counter-plot by a group of Chechen rebels or Russian officers, but, we believe that their intended actions did not take place for reasons we do not know. These people are the source of the nukes on board. They may attempt to shoot the plane down over a populated area to provoke a retaliatory strike at Moscow. Our plan, if the plane flies out over the Atlantic, is to shoot it down over deep water. Right now, we need a plane up there to ward off any attempt on the part of the

Russians or the rebels to shoot the plane down over Europe or Britain. The plane is on a bogus flight plan that gives an estimated time of arrival at Paris five hours from now. Can you do this?

Yes, I can, General. I will get our men at Aviano on this immediately. We may have to shuttle aircraft to tail this airplane because fighters do not carry enough fuel to loiter very long. Not a big problem, but something our guys will have to take care of. Flying up to the airplane with our transponders turned off, we may be able to get up there without detection, either by air traffic control or the people in the plane. I will call you back when we have a plane on the way."

"Good, Jack. I will wait your call. Good bye."

The General held the headset in his hand for a moment, distracted by the thought of what he had just put in place. He shook his head involuntarily and turned to look at the map again.

Chapter 52

The elevator carrying Lero stopped at the top deck.
It was in the galley between first class and tourist
seating. He waited a half a minute after it reached
the top deck before he tried opening the door.
When he did crack the door, he found that the galley
area was darkened, but there was a little light
coming from the sign over the emergency exit about
ten feet ahead of his station and across the fuselage
from him. Seeing no one, he opened the door and
stepped out, gripping his assault rifle at the ready.
He searched the compartment and found no one.
He went through the main passenger compartment
and found it empty of people, but strewn with the
debris left behind by the people who had been
killed. There were coats, shoes, papers, brief cases,
lap top computers, cell phones, small pieces of
carry-on luggage, drink glasses, plates and flat ware
strewn all along the cabin. There were puddles of
vomit and urine which he managed to avoid. In a
couple of minutes he had determined that there was
no one between him and the galley he had just left.
Now, to return to the galley and search the plane
forward toward the flight deck door.

In another couple of tense minutes, he reached the
forward first class lounge which was just aft of the
flight deck. The flight deck door was closed and he

could see in the gap between the door and the frame, the stainless steel latch was projecting out of the door and into the strike plate in the door frame.

He returned to the elevator and with the light switch, signaled Jean to come up. She loaded all their gear into the elevator and climbed in. It was crowded, but she came up with all the equipment they had.

They put the equipment out on the counter of the galley, so they could retrieve what they needed quickly. She drew him over near the light over the sink and took another look at his head wound. It was still steadily seeping a little blood. She took a wet towel and wiped his head.

He thanked her and kissed her.

He said, "We need to review our plan in case I begin to have symptoms. The way I see it, those two guys we shot were about to take over the plane from the pilots. We can only guess who they were and what their intentions were, but we need to focus now on the situation at hand. We have to assume that the pilots and anyone else in the flight deck are part of the original plot. These people have already killed all the passengers who were on this plane. My belief is that they removed the bodies while the plane was in the hangar at Karachi. In my opinion, they are going to try a trans-Atlantic strike on the United States. Our guys are probably following this plane on radar and perhaps otherwise and they will not let the plane reach our shores. One problem is that they do not know that we are on board. They know that we entered the hangar, but we cannot be certain that they know much more than that. We are caught on the horns of a dilemma here. We should not attempt to take the aircraft while it is over Europe or Britain because if we fail or before we succeed, they may crash the plane or detonate the nukes over a populated area. A high altitude nuclear blast would kill a lot of people and it would paralyze the power grids and fry every computer on the ground for several miles around. If I do not receive orders to do otherwise, I intend to take over from these pilots and fly the plane out over the Atlantic and ditch it over deep water. A plane this large will probably break apart on ditching, so, if we survive the ditching, we will need to get out hurriedly. Let's make sure there are flotation devices and a raft or two in different locations, so we can get to them as the fuselage fills with water. Based on the timing, it will be a night time ditching, too, which will make it more difficult. If we can take over from these guys, we will contact Jefe or Mr. Murfree and tell him in code what our intentions are and they can advise us to proceed with our plan or do what they want."

"I hate to put you in this danger, but we are here, we function well as a team and I know you will do the right thing if I lose consciousness or something. Just remember if this thing runs out of fuel that it will glide fine in a descent of about a thousand feet a minute. Keep flaps up and gear up until landing is imminent. The best way to ditch this big plane is to put the autopilot on heading hold, take off altitude hold and just let it fly itself to the water. Get out of the flight deck and strap into one of the aft facing flight attendant seats. That will give you the best chance. The flight deck windows will probably break on landing and you would be overcome with the water flow."

"I know this is a lot for you to take in like this, but I will review any of this as you need me to, but I tell you these things in case I suddenly lose consciousness."

Jean looked at him with concern and visibly shivered in anticipation.

"Since the flight deck door is locked, we will breach the door with a thermite charge. I have four of them with us. These are ignited with a fuse which has an end like the country matches we use when camping out. There is a striking surface next to the fuse. Once the fuse is lit, it will be about forty five seconds before the thermite charge goes off. It will not explode, but will produce a ball of fire that will melt the door and the lock like butter. Once the door is breached, we will enter and take the flight deck. These people have already killed hundreds of innocent people and they are highly motivated. They will not hesitate a moment to kill us or detonate the devices or crash the plane, whichever they decide to do, so we must act quickly. I have never asked you, but I don't think you have ever had to use lethal force before tonight. You were just fine below when those guys popped out of those drums. Are you OK to assault the flight deck? Can you shoot these guys without hesitation?"

She nodded and compressed her lips.

"These nine millimeter bullets will pierce the hull if they are fired directly at the hull from close range, but we will be approaching from behind these people and if you have to shoot, don't worry about hitting the radios or anything on the panel, but avoid shooting the windows if you can. The movie versions of a catastrophic decompression are overdone. It takes a pretty large hole to cause a catastrophic decompression. A few isolated bullet holes won't do it, but a window shot out would do it. If we do cause a decompression, don't panic, but get a hold of something and hang on until the air flow calms down."

This seemed to reassure her and gave her more confidence that they could shoot with less danger to themselves.

"I want you to cover me while I place the charge or charges on the door. If anyone opens the door while I am doing this, you will need to act quickly. My plan is to set the charges and wait until we think we are out over the ocean to breach the flight deck."

She nodded her understanding. She held her H &K like a pro while he took out the charges, peeled off the protective coatings and stuck them to the door and the frame.

Chapter 53

The freighter plowed slowly northward in the night. The sea was calm, by comparison, with only about one foot swells. As it wallowed over the surface, a small group of men hunched over a beat-up table in a cabin below decks.

"Our group at the hangar sent word that the plane took off about an hour ago. It will pass closest to us in about three hours, at which time, we should be about fifty miles off of the northern Italian coast. We will listen closely for orders as the flight progresses. If they feel that security is compromised, they may ask us to shoot the plane down at it approaches Paris or sooner or perhaps later as it crosses over Great Britain. The low yield warhead in the missile will not damage the weapons on board unless there is a direct hit on them, which is unlikely. Even if it hits the nuclear weapons, and they do not detonate, the hit will most probably disperse the chemical weapons over a large area. If we achieve the desired result, the plane will crash in a highly populated area."

"We will be standing by in the hold to program the missile to close with the on board tracking device," said Yosef, the oldest of the three men around the table.

"The hatch covering over the hold is in good working order and we can draw it back in about four minutes."

"Good," said Heckmatyar, the leader. "You men get some rest, but be ready to act on short notice if we get an order to fire the missile. I would expect the order in the next four hours if it comes at all."

The group dispersed and headed for their bunks to sleep a little while one kept watch.

FedEx Flight 314 flew along steadily in the night at Flight Level three two zero. It was approaching the border between Syria and Turkey southeast of Incerlik.

Chapter 54

"Heads up, you guys. Scramble two F-117s. Keep two on standby. Flight plan to follow."

"Yes sir," said the ready room communications airman.

"Hey, sir, I just received a scramble order from Ops Center. Two F-117s, two more to remain on standby."

"Holy Cow, Reynolds," said Captain Brewer. "Any clue what this is about?" he asked as he jumped up and down to wiggle into his flight suit.

"They said they would give us a flight plan once airborne."

"What is the active runway?" asked Brewer.

"Runway 7, sir," said Reynolds.

"I will get you guys current weather if you want."

"Do that, please, and call us in the planes when you get it," said Reynolds as he opened the door to sprint to the F-117 which sat in a lighted revetment which was open on both ends. As soon as they taxied out, the lights would go out.

Brewer and his wingman, Lieutenant Overley, walked quickly to their planes.

"Just need to get airborne quickly. They will brief us on the plan once airborne. You OK?"

"Yes, sir, I am good to go," said Overley.

"Good luck, then. Here we go," said Brewer as he turned toward the revetment where his plane stood ready. The ground crew was waiting for him. His crew chief was holding the ladder for him beneath the belly of the fighter.

"She's good to go, sir. All tanks topped, guns and missiles certified by the ordnance guys. Be careful up there," said Maxwell, the ground crew chief.

"Thanks, Max," said Brewer as he swung to the first rung on the ladder.

When he had settled into his cockpit seat, Brewer signaled to the ground crewman at the starter cart with a thumbs up. The ground crew man returned the signal and Brewer raised the switch to start the start cycle of the port engine.

Once both engines were turning and the gauges were coming up to the normal range, Brewer radioed the tower.

"Incerlik Tower, Badger One and Two on the east tarmac to taxi for immediate takeoff."

"Roger, Badger One, Taxi to Runway Seven. Understand there will be no squawk on departure."

"That is affirmative, Badger One," said Brewer, and raised the switch for the landing lights. The runway lights were on low intensity and the white intermittent lines on the center line of the runway gleamed in the lights of the plane. Brewer looked to his left and assured himself that Badger Two was there. He gave a thumbs up to Overley and Overley returned it. Then just after Brewer advanced his throttles, Overley did the same and the two planes vaulted down the runway in echelon formation. (Note: Echelon formation, in this case left echelon, means the aircraft to the left being a bit behind the aircraft on the right.)
In twelve seconds, they lifted their nose wheels and began to climb away from Runway 7. As the landing gear retracted, the landing lights went out and the planes were in the blackness of night.

Brewer set up a thousand feet per minute rate of climb.

The tower controller said: "Badger flight, contact Center on two fifty six decimal seven. Good evening."

"Badger flight over to two five six decimal seven. Thanks. Good night."

"Center, this is Badger One, off Runway 7, passing through five thousand, no squawk."

"Roger, Badger One, this is Center. Turn left to three five zero and climb to flight level two four zero, report reaching."

"Badger one, left to three five zero and up to two four thousand and will report," said Brewer.

In a few minutes, Brewer and Overley reached flight level two four zero and leveled off.

"Center, Badger flight is level at two four zero."

"Roger, Badger flight, contact Papa Bear on two seven three decimal three. Good evening."

Papa Bear was code for the EWACS aircraft that was orbiting at flight level three three zero about fifty nautical miles north west of Badger Flight. (AWACS aircraft are built on the same airframe as a Boeing 707) This hand-off meant that it would be directing Badger Flight until further notice.

"Papa Bear, this is Badger flight, level at two four zero."

"Badger flight, this is Papa Bear. Come up on satellite radio, channel fourteen, please and check in."

Conversations on the satellite link were scrambled and secure. Brewer switched his satellite radio to Channel fourteen.

"Papa Bear, this is Badger One."

"Roger, Badger One, this is Papa Bear. Hear you loud and clear. Stand by for flight advisories. A second voice joined the conversation on the frequency.

"Badger One, you are to shadow a Boeing seven seven seven that is about fifty miles north west of you at flight level three three zero. One of you is to approach close enough so that any radar blip will blend. Keep transponder off. Badger Two is to loiter about ten miles in trail offset to the left. The aircraft you are shadowing is a hijack. We believe it is carrying terrorists who have three Russian nukes on board that were stolen by a Chechen sympathizer in the KGB. We also think there is a quantity of chemical weapons and/or biological weapons on board. Hopefully the hijacked aircraft will continue over Europe and head for the United States. We may want you to shoot the aircraft down over deep water off the coast of Great Britain. However, if it makes a hostile gesture, like a sudden turn or sudden loss of altitude, we may want you to shoot it down before it gets to the coast. We have chemical and biological warfare squads all over Europe at the ready in case that happens. We would not expect the nukes to detonate if the plane is shot down, but the chemicals and biological agents would probably disperse. If the hijackers get wind of you tailing them, they may set off the nukes to wipe out every computer within a hundred miles, not to mention killing hundreds of thousands of people on the ground. It may be that the weapons are already armed and set to explode when the aircraft descends to a previously determined altitude. You will loiter with the aircraft and will be relieved when you reach bingo fuel. Have you clearly heard this briefing, so far?"

(Note;: "Bingo fuel is enough fuel to return to base.)

"Yes sir, Badger One heard every word," said Brewer.

"Badger Two, likewise," said Overley.

Chapter 55

Lero said to Jean: "I want you to stay here and watch the door carefully. If they open the door, remember, our job here is to take the aircraft. If you can successfully shoot all the occupants of the flight deck, then do it. If you have to shoot, I will hear and come immediately. I am going to open the nuclear device containers and see if they are armed and possibly pre-set to detonate at a given latitude and longitude or altitude. OK?"

Jean nodded and gave his arm a squeeze. She asked him: "Let me shine the flashlight in your eyes to see if you pupils look normal. I will turn it on low."

Lero nodded his agreement.

Jean shown the flashlight on his eyes, one at a time. She also looked at the wound in his scalp. It was not bleeding.

She said: "Your eyes look normal. Please be alert for any change in sensory capacity or fuzzy thinking. There is no way to tell how far that bullet penetrated, but I don't think it penetrated very far. Please be careful. If you are not back in ten minutes, I will come after you."

Lero nodded his agreement and patted her shoulder as he rose and went aft.

The devices were on separate pallets. Each pallet was made of wood, about eight feet long by four feet wide and thicker than a standard pallet, probably eight inches thick. Each of the devices were strapped to the pallet with ratcheting straps and each had a rack under it to interface between the cylindrical shape of the device and the flat upper surface of the pallet. The racks were fastened to the pallets with bolts. The containers appeared to be made of stainless steel. There were Cyrillic characters and numbers on each device, clearly indicating that they were Russian, or rather, Soviet, in design.

The containers had eight snap fasteners along each side. The fasteners were of "over-center" design and popped loose as soon as the handle was pulled a certain distance. There was a rubber gasket around the entire mating surface of the bottom half of each container to seal it. When Lero opened the first container, it gave off an odor of rubber and plastic which dissipated quickly. There was a small hatch on the side of the device. It had a Dzus type fastener, like on the luggage door of a Cessna 182, he thought. When he pressed it inward, it unlatched the hatch which opened on a hinge. Inside was a series of toggle switches, a five inch by seven inch computer screen and an LED screen as well as several individual LED lit buttons.

Lero was thankful for the Russian language lessons he had taken after he came to Davis Monthan to join Jefe. The code to command "Read Settings" was stenciled in black paint on the light gray background. After he had read all the words on the panel inside the hatch and on the inside of the hatch, he pressed the numbers to tell the onboard computer that he wanted to read the settings. He was relieved to see the display show that the device was not armed, but just below that message were the words: "Allow remote settings." Lero knew then that the pilots and any others on the flight deck could set the settings on the devices from the flight deck using a device to communicate with the devices. While his inspection gained information, it left open the question of what the intent of the hijackers was. They could easily detonate the devices, or preset them to detonate at a given latitude and longitude or at a pre-determined altitude as the aircraft descended, or indeed, at a pre-determined time or after a pre-determined amount of time. He saw no way in which he could disable the device, so he closed the hatch and checked the others. He found them all set the same way. As he stood up to return to Jean, he noticed that he was a bit light-headed.

In a minute, he signaled Jean that he was approaching with his flashlight and then went forward to her.

"The nuclear devices are not armed, but are set so that they can be set and armed remotely. I expect they have a remote device in the flight deck that they can use to tell the devices how they want them to detonate. This makes taking the flight deck quickly very important. None of them can be allowed to program the devices, so we need to act quickly once we start."

Jean nodded her acknowledgement. She shifted her H & K assault rifle to a more comfortable position by her side and gave Lero a quick kiss.

"Papa Bear, Badger flight, in position."

"Roger, Badger One."

The commander lifted his secure phone.

"Ramparts, this is Zebra control. Badger One is in position."

In less than a minute, the phone rang on the desk beside the President. His military aide picked it up.

"Yes," was his short response to the ring.

"I see. Thank you."

Sir, Zebra Control reports that Badger One and Two are in position."

"Very good, thank you," said the President as he continued to scowl at the budget print out on his desk.

"I wonder why we have not heard from Lero," he thought. "Hope he is okay."

"Now we have the capability to shoot the aircraft down. But if the hijackers decide to detonate the nukes, the pilots of Badger flight will be instantly incinerated," he thought.

Chapter 56

"FedEx three one four, Zurich control."

"This is FedEx three one four, go ahead Zurich."

"You are entering our airspace, squawk 2275 please."

"FedEx three one four, squawking 2275, level at Flight level three three zero."

"Roger, three one four, maintain flight level three three zero."

"Three one four, Roger."

Three one four was now about sixty nautical miles south east of Zurich, following its previously filed bogus flight plan. Paris was now about an hour and a half ahead.

"Paris Center, this is Zurich Center. Handing off FedEx Flight three one four, now at Flight level three three zero in your Bezancon sector."

"Roger, Zurich Center, will accept the hand-off. Thanks."

Chapter 57

Aboard Russian nuclear submarine Kirsk II, the communications officer received a message through the antenna extended on a tether to the surface.

"TO: Captain Konovolov, Commander of Kirsk II

Believe Chechen rebels have stolen three Type KB-7 Nuclear weapons and with assistance of ISIS forces have hijacked a Boeing 777. Chemical or biological weapons also believed to be aboard. Aircraft is approaching Paris on a forged Federal Express flight plan. Make all available speed southwest immediately. Ready missiles for an aerial strike. If aircraft appears to be heading for the United States, we will want you to shoot it down over the Atlantic. Premier believes U. S. will mistakenly retaliate against us if these weapons are detonated over U. S. territory. Confirm receipt of this message."

When Captain Konovolov read the message, he immediately instructed his Executive Officer, Major Malenkov to place the boat at battle stations and order all available speed on a course of two two zero degrees. At that time, the submarine was four hundred nautical miles north of Glasgow.

Using the satellite link for security purposes, General Behm had the communications officer send the following message to Badger One: "Believe Russian submarine may try to shoot the Boeing 777 down with a missile. Take appropriate action to intercept missile if possible."

Badger One moved from a trailing position to a position slightly behind and just to the right of the right wingtip of the 777. Badger Two moved up to a position just behind and to the left of the left wingtip. Brewer noticed that he had four thousand pounds of fuel left, enough to loiter at this position for another forty five minutes.

Badger One noticed the F-117 off of his left. There had been no radio communication to tell him that he was being relieved, but he knew his time on station was ending because his fuel level was now eighteen hundred pounds, enough to get him home, but not a lot to spare. He rocked his wings to signal the other F-117 that he saw him and began a slow descent. When he was a thousand feet below the 777, he glanced up to see his relief F-117 slide into position just aft of the right wingtip of the 777. By now, Badger Two had formed up with him behind and to the left. He rocked his wings and, after a brief hesitation, began a shallow turn to the right. His DME showed Mendenhall was two hundred eighty nautical miles. (DME stands for Distance Measuring Equipment, it tells the pilot the distance from or to a navigation radio on the ground and can tell ground speed also. The military name for this equipment is TACAN.)

Chapter 58

General Behm asked his aide to get the President on the line. In a minute or so, the aide reached out the headset to General Behm and nodded.

"Mr. President?" he asked.

"Yes, General Behm, what do you have?"

"Well, sir, there is another contingency that I thought of, realizing that this situation is very flexible. What if the Russians, in their paranoia, decide to shoot the aircraft down so the nukes do not detonate, but which would disperse the chemical or biological agents? What if they do that over Europe? They can claim that the nukes were stolen from them and they were trying to prevent the detonation of the nukes in Europe or on U.S. soil. The canisters of chemical or biological agents will have markings that indicate either Iraqi or Syrian manufacture, we believe."

"Are our fighters still in formation with the hijacked aircraft?" asked the President.

"Yes, sir, but just as a precaution, I think we had better alert any of our submarines in the Mediterranean or off the western shore of Europe to be ready to shoot down any intruding Russian attack aircraft or missiles."

"Do we have any Patriot batteries or Iron Dome batteries that could reach a missile heading for that plane on its present course?" asked the President.

"Yes, we do, Mr. President. There is another thought about the situation, if I may."

"Sure, go ahead, Arnold," said the President.

"The Russians may want to shoot the plane down to prevent it from hitting us and us
retaliating against them. It may be that is doing so, they would deprive the Chechens of
their intended effect. It would also conceal any evidence that the nukes were theirs.

"I see," said the President. "This really is complicated, isn't it? Keep me in touch, Arnold."

Chapter 59

Lero said to Jean: "I think I am beginning to have symptoms. Watch me closely. I don't think we should wait too much longer to assault the flight deck. I had hoped to wait until we were over the Atlantic west of England, but we may not be able to wait. I want to be able to help you fly this plane as long as possible."

"Help me fly this plane?" asked Jean. "If this weren't such a serious situation, I would think you were joking."

"I am not joking. I felt a bit light headed back there when I stood up after checking the nukes. I just wanted to give you a heads up. I feel OK for now, but I sense a bit of wooziness. Just watch me closely," he said.

A few seconds after that conversation, the flight deck door opened and a man stepped out. He did not look at them, perhaps confident that there were no other people on board. As he turned to enter the lavatory, Lero lunged quickly at him and hit him over the back of the head with his assault rifle stock. The man crumpled and lay still. Lero quickly dragged him away from the flight deck door and tied his ankles and wrists with plastic tie wraps. Then he tied his ankles to the anchor of a nearby passenger seat, so he would be restrained in place. He put duct tape over his mouth, then returned to Jean.

"That is one less person we have to overcome to take the flight deck. There may be several more. They may have a stand-by crew since it is such a long flight. I think we should plan on assaulting the flight deck when someone comes out to look for this man. He did not see the thermite charge, so I am going to leave it in place. We may not be so lucky the next time."

Sure enough, in about fifteen minutes, another man came out the door. Lero grabbed him by his right arm and flung him out onto the deck. As he sprang to his feet to attack Lero, Jean shot him twice with her H & K assault rifle. Lero quickly went through the flight deck door. By now the others inside had grabbed their pistols or other weapons and were turning to confront him. He shot the pilot and first officer with two bursts just as they fired at him. One bullet hit Lero near the bottom of his protective vest, knocking him back momentarily. Just as he hit the bulkhead, another man came from the door to the stand-by crew bunk room. Lero shot him while he still had his back to the bulkhead. The door to the stand-by crew bunk room stood open. Lero approached cautiously, his finger on the trigger of his assault rifle. When he peeked around the door jamb, he saw that the other crew man had been hit by a stray round from the shots he fired at the pilots or that they had fired at him. There was a neat hole in his left temple and blood was running from a large exit wound over his right ear.

Lero quickly checked over the flight instruments and radios. Since the radios were in the console between the seats of the pilots, they had no damage, but there were several bullet holes in the panel and instruments. One bullet had hit the gear lever handle, shattering it. The co-pilot's directional gyro had a neat hole near the middle and was kaput. Another bullet had hit one of the engine warning lights in front of the pilot and it was dimly glowing and smoking a little. There were no holes or hits on any of the windshield panels, for which Lero was very grateful. Also luckily, the autopilot was not damaged. The big plane motored on into the night as if nothing had happened.

He went back out into the cabin and found Jean with her assault rifle pointed at the door he came through. She indicated relief that it was he who came out and lowered her weapon.

He said: "I think that is all of them. I will drag their bodies out of their seats. I may need to bring some out here. I will need your help."

Jean nodded and followed him back into the flight deck. They pulled the stand-by pilot's body back into the passenger cabin and rolled it to the side of the aisle. The pilot's body was pulled back enough to clear the path to the pilot's seat and pushed to the side. The co-pilot's body, they had to drag out to the passenger cabin.

Once Lero and Jean got the bodies out of the way, they went forward and climbed into the pilots' seats, being careful to lock the flight deck door, just in case. Lero put his assault rifle on the console to his right, with the muzzle facing aft, too.

"First, we need to find out where we are," said Lero.

The first navigation radio was set on one one four decimal two. Lero put on his earphones and turned up the volume. The Morse code identifier came through clearly. "L" "N" "D".

"That radio is on the Land's End VOR-DME. We are on the two three zero radial from it and the DME reads three eight five. We are about three hundred eighty five nautical miles south west of Land's End which is the most south west land mass in Britain. We are over the Atlantic southwest of England. Thank God!! Now, we need to contact our people and tell them where we are and let them tell us where they want us to land. While I am getting things sorted out, go look for the arming equipment. It may be a laptop computer or a device about that size. When you find it, bring it here so we can decide what to do."

Jean nodded and got out of her seat to go look for the arming device.

Chapter 60

Within a minute of the warning, Lieutenant DeFino, Brewer's relief, saw the missile threat warning light blare in bright red. His radar warned that the missile was at their four o'clock position, fifty miles out and climbing through flight level two four zero. He turned to the right to intercept the missile. He did not have enough time to fire any of his own missiles, though. With a closing speed of Mach 4, the missile was coming too fast to be intercepted. He watched with growing fear as the tail of flame came at him. He could see the flame behind the missile, but could not make out the missile itself.

The on-board armament system in the missile had been set for "proximity" which meant that it did not have to actually hit anything to detonate its warhead. If it sensed the proximity of a metal object, such as an aircraft, it would detonate.

In the brief interlude from the first moment he spotted the missile and realized that he had not chance to dodge it, De Fino said a brief prayer and thought of his sweet wife so far away. He readied himself to die like a modern aviator, high in the sky where it was sixty below and going the speed that he was going, he would not survive a minute. He stared in wonder as the missile closed with his F-117. Then just as he expected to be blown to smithereens, the missile passed beneath him and detonated about two hundred yards beyond him. Evidently the sensors had been confused by the close formation of the F-117 and the Boeing 777 about four hundred yards now behind Brewer. There was a blinding flash of light and he felt the impact of a tremendous explosion. The aircraft was blown in two just aft of the cockpit and he spun into the darkness He had been going about four hundred fifty knots almost northerly away from the Boeing. Now, he was slowing up, but plummeting toward the ocean still at more than three hundred knots. In spite of the G-forces pulling at him, he managed to pull the protective hood off of the ejection arming switch and flip the switch upward. There was another blinding flash of light and he was catapulted into blackness again.

The blast that blew his F-117 in two partially crushed the fuselage of the Boeing 777. Numerous small holes and rents in the metal skin caused the big aircraft to experience a catastrophic loss of pressure. Lero and Jean were strapped into their seats, but everything loose in the aircraft was caught in a stream of rapidly moving air. As the air moved to leave the pressurized fuselage, it was like a rapidly moving stream. White water. In ten seconds, though, it was over. The fuselage was filled with a fog of condensing moisture in the air as the air began to cool to well below zero. Lero reached back and grabbed his quick donning oxygen mask. Jean saw him do that and reached for hers, too. Lero, true to his training, reduced thrust on both engines and put the gigantic aircraft into a descent, not too rapid for fear that the structural damage done by the missile would cause the airplane to rip apart. He slowed the aircraft to a moderate speed for structural reasons. There was no need to get to altitudes where they could breathe atmospheric oxygen since they had the masks to supply their needs. So, he continued to slow the aircraft as it descended. He turned transmitter number one to one hundred twenty one decimal five kilohertz, the International Emergency Frequency.

"Papa Bear, if you hear me this is Lero. Repeat. This is Lero. We are onboard the Boeing 777 and in control for the moment. Three souls on board, including one unconscious terrorist, plus three deceased terrorists. Descending out of flight level one niner zero. We have major structural damage due to missile detonation nearby. Many holes in the fuselage. Engine number two is spooling down, its oil temp gauge is reading hot, not producing any power. See no alternative but to ditch. Transponder has been off, but will now turn it on and squawk 4444. Request you attempt to get to us quickly once we ditch. If we survive the ditching, we will be glad to see you guys. God Bless America."

He looked over to Jean and spoke to her on the intercom in their headsets.

"I want you to go aft. Get out the inflatable rafts. Inflate one in the passenger compartment. We may use that one if the fuselage ruptures on ditching. If we don't break apart on ditching, we will use another one that we can inflate once we get in the water. Find a seat that faces aft. If you cannot find a seat that faces aft, get behind a bulkhead and cushion your head with a pillow or something. We are going to hit hard. I expect the fuselage to break aft of the wings. With all the mass of this aircraft, it will take a while for it to come to rest. Do not worry if it comes to rest under water. Hold onto the inflated raft and ride it to the surface. If you have time, get a rope from my bag and tie one end to my right ankle and the other end around your ankle. Keep a knife handy in case you need to cut me or yourself loose. Cut the prisoner's legs loose from the seat anchor. If he wakes up, he can swim to the surface. We have about ten minutes before we hit the water. I am going to have my hands full up here, so once you have me tied off, don't come back into the flight deck."

"I am sorry I got you into this, Jean. I love you so much. Thanks for your help and thank you for being so sweet to me."

She got out of her seat like he told her to. She came over and kissed him firmly. Then, she wrenched herself out between the seats and went aft.

The earphones crackled: "Lero this is Papa Bear. Message received. Have helicopters enroute from the Bon Homme Richard. Estimate your ditching location to be four hundred ten miles south west of Liverpool. Ocean surface conditions are: air temp ten Celcius, water temperature eight Celcius, swells are four feet or less, wind is from two eight five degrees at eleven knots, altimeter setting is two niner niner seven. Good luck. No matter what happens, thank you and Jean for what you have done. Papa Bear standing by."

As they passed through ten thousand feet, Jean appeared and tied the end of the black nylon rope around Lero's right ankle. She put a rescue flotation device around his arm, where he could get into it after ditching. Then she hugged his neck and went aft to find a place to brace for the ditching. Lero moved the trim wheel to raise the nose of the big plane into a glide speed of one hundred eighty knots. He noticed that the vertical speed indicator showed a steady eleven hundred feet per minute rate. In eight minutes they would be in the water. He turned to a heading of two eight five to land into the wind. This would assure the minimum speed of the aircraft over the water as they landed.   He knew that the plane had about one fourth of its fuel yet on board, enough to have reached the United States. He quickly calculated his approach speed at that weight. Like most ditchings, he decided to land with full flaps, but with the landing gear up. He thought that if the plane landed nose down too much, the water would break the wind shield panels and drown him before he could escape. If he hit the water just right, the windshields would be about thirty five feet above the surface, though. He turned the knob on the altimeter to set its pressure to two niner niner seven, so it would accurately tell him how high he was above the water. He watched as the altimeter continued to unwind, now at five thousand six hundred feet. A quick glance showed that he was a little fast, so he added a bit more nose up trim.

He thought to himself: "So this is how it feels to have your life flash before your eyes."

He remembered Jean in the cabin behind him and how much he loved her. He remembered how dear she was to wake up with. He remembered how she had looked standing in the bathroom doorway that first time she asked him to help her with her "all over moisturizer." Then he shook himself back into concentration and checked the heading indicator once more. Two eight seven. He gave it a tiny bit of left rudder and checked the airspeed again. One seven eight. Good to go. The altitude was one thousand eight hundred now. "Here we go," he thought. "Lord help us."

Chapter 61

The whole approach was surreal. There was enough ambient light from the quarter moon and the stars for him to see the ocean's surface when he passed through a thousand feet. He hit the flap lever and brought the nose up with more trim. The big plane shuddered at the deployment of the flaps. He noticed that the airspeed was decaying rapidly, but there was no use in trying to adjust it just now. The big plane passed through the last thousand feet quicker than he was used to. Just before they hit, he pulled back on the yoke to give the plane just a bit more of nose up attitude. He pushed his seat back as far as it would go, put his foot on the panel and pulled the yoke all the way back. There was a tremendous splash of water over the nose of the aircraft as it hit. The deceleration was immediate and forceful. His arms splayed out ahead of him and his body strained against the seat belts. He felt them dig into him. The deceleration continued for twenty seconds or so. It seemed like a week. Lero could not see the huge splash of water that cascaded up over the nose of the airplane and from its wings as it hit the water. He heard a tremendous rending sound as the tail section of the Boeing separated aft of the wings like he thought it would. The right wing caught in the waves and the giant plane spun to the right before coming to a halt in a huge splash. It had traveled over a thousand feet since it first touched the water. He could see nothing but blackness out the windshields. He thought that they were sinking and felt true fright. But, as he shook himself to recover from the stresses of the ditching, he noticed the water's surface appear in the windshields as the nose section regained the surface. He knew this temporary respite would not last long, so as soon as he could, he unfastened his seat belt harness and tried to climb out of his seat. His legs felt wooden and would not obey his will to stand up.

He could not see it, but water a foot deep was pouring over the floor of the passenger compartment. It would only speed up as the nose filled and tilted more downward.

The first splash of ocean water startled him. The plane had only been in the water less than a minute and water was already reaching into the flight deck. He could still move his arms, so he decided when he could float, he would swim aft and try to get out. As the water level reached his waist, he tried again to get out of the seat. His legs stubbornly refused to help him. Within a few seconds, the water reached his shoulders and he felt himself beginning to grow lighter on his seat. Just then, Jean appeared beside him. She did not speak, but just grabbed his right arm and heaved him upward. She got a good foot hold on the console and wrestled him upward some. He could now reach the hand hold on the overhead that pilots use to ease themselves into and out of the seat. Together, they managed to get him out into the fast filling flight deck. In moments, they were floating where they should have been walking. They swam toward the broken open end of the fuselage. As they struggled aft, the fuselage filled completely and they took a quick breath and swam as hard as they could. It got very dark and they had no directional advice from any light. They swam for about forty seconds before they popped to the surface. It was strangely quiet and there was no fire, but there was a strong smell of jet fuel. The water had a greasy feel to it and Lero knew that they were in a surface pool of jet fuel. They continued to swim and in a minute or so, the water changed character and they felt they were out of the jet fuel. The only thing left showing on the surface of the ocean from the plane was about ten feet of the left wing tip. The rest had submerged. There was evidently enough empty space in the wing fuel tanks to give the wreckage enough buoyancy to float for a while like that.

After they had floated for a few minutes, Jean spotted the inflatable raft about a hundred yards from them. They began a slow swim toward it. It took all of twenty minutes to reach the raft. When they got hold of the ropes on the top of the outer inflated parts, Jean pulled herself into the boat and rested a couple of minutes, then she helped Lero into the boat. With both of them pulling with their arms, they pulled him over the side into the boat like a large fish.

They thankfully collapsed into the raft, not speaking for a while. When they both had rested for several minutes, Lero said: "I would not have made it without your help. Thanks."

She hugged him and said: "The important thing is that we made it. We need to get you to a hospital."

He nodded his agreement.

Chapter 62

In about twenty minutes, they heard the first sounds of a helicopter. The Sea Stallion materialized out of the dark and turned on its landing lights when it was about a thousand feet from them. Once the lights played on the raft, it hovered about thirty feet above the surface. The downwash was tremendous. Water stung their faces. It halted about thirty yards from them and a diver came out of the side hatch and dove into the water. They watched in fatigued amazement as he swam to them. He was dragging the shoulder harness from the helicopter and it took him a while to get it and himself over to the raft.

When he got close, he said: "Good evening, who goes first?" Jean said: "Take him first. He has a head wound and needs to get to a hospital quickly."

The diver nodded and began putting the shoulder harness around Lero. Lero was not able to help him much. When the harness was in place, the diver gave a hand signal to the crewman in the hatch of the helicopter and the line tightened. Then the diver held onto Lero's left leg to help him line up as the line lifted him free of the raft. The diver and Jean watched as Lero was hoisted up to the helicopter. Two strong arms reached out and pulled Lero in. Jean and the diver could not see it, but the crew men helped Lero to a seat on the forward bulkhead of the bay and strapped him in. Then they appeared again at the open hatch and lowered the harness again. The diver helped Jean into the harness once they got hold of it. Jean twisted a full three hundred sixty degrees twice on the trip up to the helicopter. The crewmen helped her out of the harness and over to a seat beside Lero on the forward bulkhead. She strapped in and gave his arm a pat. He patted her leg and smiled.

In a couple of minutes, the rescue diver came on board and, as soon as he strapped in, the big helicopter began to move over the water. In a minute, they were going a hundred and twenty knots toward the Bon Homme Richard.

The flight took about twenty five minutes. When the Sea Stallion landed on the Bon Homme Richard, there were plenty of helpers to get Lero and Jean and the crew members out. The line men pulled the helicopter over to the elevator and took the big thing below. Corpsmen put Lero on a stretcher and carried him to Sick Bay. Jean followed. Once Jean told them how he had been shot and by what, they took X-ray pictures of his skull and found that a small bullet had lodged between his skull and the dura mater that surrounds the brain. In twenty minutes, Lero was under anesthesia. Jean waited patiently in the waiting room, nursing a large cup of hot chocolate.

"We will keep him over night," said the Doctor after he came out to report to her about how the surgery went. "We found some bruising and bleeding beneath the dura and evacuated it all. He should make a complete recovery, but have him take it easy for a couple of weeks. Watch for any balance problems and report to a hospital if he loses consciousness or falls. He is one lucky guy to have you with him, ma'am."

"It was important to him and to all of us that he was able to stay capable long enough to ditch the plane, but I don't think he could have lasted much longer," she said.

"Well, that is behind you both now. That must have been pretty hairy work up there. Do you have any residual damage from the bullet strike?" he asked.

"I have a large bruise about an inch wide and five inches long across my lower rib cage, but other than that, I am okay," she said.

"If you need some pain medication, I could prescribe it," said Doctor Travis.

"Not now, thanks," she said, "but could you give me a pill or two in case it wakes me up in the middle of the night?"

"Sure," he said, and he turned to his orderly and told him to tell the pharmacy mate to give her four Tramadol tablets.

"There is a Mr. Murfree who has been calling on the satellite phone for either of you. When you are ready to take the call, just let one of these people know and they will get you a phone."

Jean dozed off for a while. When she awoke, the clock on the wall indicated that she had slept for forty five or so minutes.

She signaled to the chief behind the counter at the far end of the room.

"I could take that phone call now, if it is convenient," she said.

He lifted his phone and spoke to someone for a moment. Then he said to her, "It will be just a minute. A seaman will bring you the satellite phone and he will wait to take it back when you are finished."

Sure enough, in about three minutes, a young red headed seaman, who did not look a day over sixteen, came in, came to attention and said: "Seaman Walter Jones, with your telephone, ma'am." He handed it to her like it was dozen eggs.

Jean put the receiver to her ear. "Hello," she said. The deep voice of President Thompson came through the earpiece. "Say the word, please," he said.

"Sonora," she said. Now they both knew whom they were talking to.

"How are you and how is Lero?" asked the President.

"Lero had a head wound in the skirmish to take the flight deck. He was bleeding some, but did not appear to be badly wounded. The Doctor says he had a subdural hematoma where the bullet pierced his skull and lodged outside of the dura mater. He was lucky. We thought the bullet was a ricochet from the encounter. The Doctor says they will keep him in recovery overnight, but he thinks Lero will be fine after some rest. He said for him to take it really easy for a couple of weeks. I am fine except for some bruises and scrapes, but sore all over."

"Jean, I cannot tell you how grateful we are for what you and Lero did. We had no way of knowing for sure that you were on board. The last information we had was from Rangit who said you both went into the hangar and after that we had no information. Some time you both need to tell me how you got into the aircraft and managed to avoid detection. Please tell Lero how grateful I am. Both of you get some rest and I want to see you sometime soon.

I am sorry that you both had to use lethal force. It was necessary, of course. Those people would have killed you and Lero in an instant if they could have.

I received word that our submarine West Virginia reached the crash site about an hour after you all were rescued. GPS coordinates enabled it to find it right away. Since it was still floating, divers went on board the plane and removed the three nuclear weapons. It was felt that the best disposition of the chemical weapons was to sink the airplane wreckage with them in it. Our men got good underwater photos of the markings on the chemical weapons canisters, so we have proof where they came from.

I want you and Lero to come to Washington sometime soon and visit with me. Although we cannot talk publicly about what you all did, I want to hear your description of the events and visit with you both some."

The public will be informed that the U.S. Navy located the sinking wreckage of the airliner and that all of the passengers and crew are, regrettably, dead. We will say that the aircraft broke apart upon hitting the water and sank just as our ship reached it. We will say that a search for bodies will be mounted right away. We do not intend to reveal the location of the wreckage, but will report that it sank in deep water in the Indian Ocean.

I cannot tell you how grateful we are to you and Lero. Take good care of him and give him my best regards when he awakens. See you soon, Jean."

"Thank you, Mister President. See you soon."

The line disconnected.

Jean motioned to the seaman who had gone out into the hall so as not to overhear the conversation in obedience to his chief's instructions. He came promptly and took the phone.

Chapter 63

It was about six in the morning, local time when Lero stirred and awakened from the anesthesia and pharmaceuticals. The first thing he saw was the white ceiling of the Sick Bay. The next thing he saw was Jean's face looking down at him. When she saw that he was awake, she bent over and kissed him.

He did not speak for a moment. Then, when he did speak, his throat was dry and his mouth was dry, too, and he did not speak clearly. He said: "So good to see you. How did I do? What do they think?"

Jean sobbed and put her head on his chest. He felt her hair fall across his face and closed his eyes in gratitude.

"Dr. Connally says you are going to be fine, but you may have some residual effects for a few days or a week or so, mostly from the surgery and the anesthesia. He said it was a close call. Something about being hard headed helped, too."

Lero smiled at her and moved his right hand to touch her.

"We are going to stay on the ship for a few days so they can watch you and when they think you are able, we will be flown home. Mr. Murfree said to tell you he cannot express his gratitude. He was very worried about us. Rangit told him that we went into the hangar and that he had not heard from us again."

"How long was I out?" asked Lero.

"You came out of surgery about 10:30 last night. You were under for about two hours. They kept you sedated so you would rest over night."

The corpsman appeared and said, "Ah, Mister Lero, so good to see you awake. Are you in pain?"

"No, actually, I feel pretty good," said Lero.

"Are you hungry or thirsty? I can get you some Navy chow and a drink if you like. The Doctor said you should push fluids today."

"Sure, I could eat. May I have a large glass of orange juice? What is for breakfast?"

"You can pick from a bowl of oatmeal, scrambled eggs and sausage or bacon, or pancakes and sausage or bacon."

"Tough choice. I will try scrambled eggs and sausage. Thanks."

"You rest now and I will bring it right away. What for you, Missus Jean?"

"I will have the same, but with a cup of coffee, thanks."

Lero looked over at her and saw how concerned she had been and how relieved she was now and he sobbed.

"I am getting too old for this stuff, don't you think?"

"Actually, I do, but your age was a good disguise when we confronted that soldier at the hangar. I think if you had been younger, he would have been suspicious. Having a middle aged woman like me with you helped, too. He must have thought we looked harmless."

Just then the corpsman came in with two large trays of breakfast. The food smelled great and he had brought some biscuits and honey, too.

Lero and Jean took their time and had a nice breakfast.

They watched Fox News on the flat screen television on the wall of sick bay as they ate.

"This is Fletcher Donnally of the British Broadcasting Corporation. An undersea earthquake of a magnitude of three point eight was reported today about three hundred miles west of Liverpool on the bed of the Atlantic Ocean. Ships in the vicinity were warned to take precautions in case of a tsunami. A similar warning was issued for all of the west coast of Great Britain. So far there are no reports of damage to shipping or to the coastal communities of Great Britain. Experts say that Atlantic seabed earthquakes in the area are quite rare. Scientists at the Woods Hole Naval Observatory in Massachusetts said that their vessel Explorer was about a hundred nautical miles west of the epicenter of the quake and made recordings for later study."

They looked at each other and smiled.

Chapter 64

It was a beautiful autumn afternoon when their Grumman G-V touched down at Andrews Air Force Base. The waiting car drove them through the beautiful country side into Washington. The leaves had turned and were magnificent.

As they pulled up to the portico of the White House, President Thompson stepped out to greet them. No photographers were present. They went into the Oval Office for a visit.

When they went into the Oval Office, the President motioned them to sit opposite him on the sofas. He saw to it that they were alone, not even the White House Photographer was present. There would be time for a photo later.

"The Russians shot the plane down. They used a missile from a nuclear sub off the British coast. They did it to prevent the plane from striking our east coast because of their paranoid fear that we would retaliate without delay and wipe out their country and because the nukes were of their manufacture, even if they were stolen by Chechen separatists. So it was to avoid blame that they did it. By the way, Lieutenant DeFino survived and was picked up by one of our submarines. His wing man had his aircraft's windows blown out and some other structural damage, but was able to limp to a British airport near the west coast."

"Even now, we are not completely sure of the origin of the plot. What we believe is that the plot originated with some Islamic fanatics in the Pakistani Intelligence Service with help from Iran. It is strange, surprising and eye opening that the Pakistanis would cooperate with the Iranians, but hatred for us has caused some frightening alliances among those in Asia and the Middle East. After the airplane was ditched, we had a company of commandos storm the hangar in Karachi. Most of the bad guys got away, but we managed to catch a few medium sized fish. The whole thing will give our intel guys something to work on for some time to come."

"If it had not been for you two, we would have had to shoot the airplane down and the nukes may have detonated, not to mention scattering the chemical weapons on board. The public will never know the part you both played in this venture. All I can say is that on behalf of the United States of America, we thank you."

"Speaking of intelligence gathering, my cook has acquired the recipe from the Senate dining room cook for his bean soup recipe. Let's have some lunch."